Somehow Ginger stumbled onward, being sick again in the wastebasket by the door. Finally she was outside. The fresh air made her feel better, but it didn't stop her awful embarrassment. She wished she could die.

"Feel better?" her teacher asked.

Ginger nodded. "I'm so sorry."

"It's not your fault, Ginger. These things happen to everyone at one time or another."

Yeah, Ginger thought. At her old school, a girl named Victoria Bates had thrown up one recess, and everyone had called her Victoria Vomit the rest of the year. . . .

OFF TO A
NEW START

The Ginger Series
by Elaine L. Schulte

Here Comes Ginger!
Off to a New Start
* A Job for an Angel
* Absolutely Green

* *Coming soon*

OFF TO A NEW START

Elaine L. Schulte

Chariot Books™
David C. Cook Publishing Co.

A White Horse Book
Published by Chariot Books,™
an imprint of David C. Cook Publishing Co.
David C. Cook Publishing Co., Elgin, Illinois
David C. Cook Publishing Co., Weston, Ontario

OFF TO A NEW START
© 1989 by Elaine L. Schulte

Cover design by Ad/Plus, Ltd.
Cover illustration by Janice Skivington
First printing, 1989
Printed in the United States of America
93 92 91 90 89   5 4 3 2 1

Library of Congress Cataloging-in-Publication Data

Schulte, Elaine, L.
   Off to a new start / Elaine L. Schulte.
      p. cm.—(A Ginger book) (A White horse book)
   Summary: Having resigned herself to accepting her mother's
remarriage, ten-year-old Ginger prays for God's help in adjusting to
her new family and in switching to the Christian school where her
stepfather is principal. Sequel to "Here Comes Ginger."
   ISBN 1-55513-771-7
   [1. Remarriage—Fiction. 2. Schools—Fiction. 3. Christian life-
Fiction.]   I. Title   II. Series: Schulte, Elaine L. Ginger book.
PZ7.S3867OF   1989
[Fic.—dc19   88-35035
                                                        CIP
                                                        AC

to my friends at
Santa Fe Christian School

1

Chewing her gum slowly, Ginger brushed the green Magic Marker over her left thumbnail. There. That was it. The ghastly green color now covered all ten of her fingernails, and it looked almost as ghastly as she felt.

Outside, the car doors had already slammed, which meant in just minutes she'd have to leave Gram's house to live with her mother—and new stepfather and his kids.

"They're here, Ginger!" Gram called out from the living room. "Here come the newlyweds!"

Ginger fanned her nails. She was tempted to look at herself in the bedroom mirror, but resisted. As much as life had changed this summer, she knew she didn't look different: freckles, green eyes, tangled red curls, and straight-up-and-down shape. She was even wearing her familiar brown shorts and T-shirt, though they were a tighter fit than they used to be.

The screen door banged, and she heard Gram say, "Welcome back to southern California sunshine! Don't you two look happy! You must have had a good trip."

Voices jumbled together, then she heard her mother.

"Where's Ginger? I thought she'd be waiting out on the porch for us."

"Ginger?" her grandmother called out. "The last I saw, she was closing up her suitcase."

Ginger took a deep breath. "Coming!"

Her heart thumped loudly as she lugged her suitcase through the hallway. She could hear Gram saying, "Ginger and I had such a good time. You know, she's truly changed. She didn't lose her temper once all week."

"You mean Ginger didn't snap?" her mother asked, and they all laughed.

Ginger stepped into the living room, which was piled with colorful fabrics and half-sewn clothes from Gram's seamstress work. She pretended she hadn't heard their same old joke.

"And here she is—Ginger Anne Trumbell!" Gram announced.

Ginger grinned a little. "Hi," she said.

Setting down her suitcase, she eyed them quickly.

Mom looked beautiful as ever, with her dimples and blue eyes and brownish-red hair. Her stepfather, Grant Gabriel, had his arm around Mom, and his grayish-blue eyes were bright with happiness.

"I've missed you so much, Ginger," Mom said, hurrying to her. "Give me a hug."

Ginger's eyes clouded as her mother held her. "I missed you, too, Mom." She'd never been away from her for a whole week. They'd spent nearly every day together for the last three years, since her parents' divorce.

Mom held Ginger at arm's length. "Let me see you." As her eyes wandered down, her smile faded. "Your nails are green again! Oh, Ginger, you're almost eleven—"

They all stared, and Ginger gave her gum a loud crack.

Grant chuckled. "Well, Ginger," he said, "green is still your best color."

"Why did you do that?" Gram asked. She shook her head, and her short salt-and-pepper curls shone in the sunlit room.

Ginger shrugged and chewed her gum hard.

Grant stepped forward with a large plastic shopping bag. "We brought you a special gift from Seattle."

"For me?" Ginger asked. Had they really thought about her while they were on their honeymoon?

"Open it," her mother urged.

Ginger peered into the bag, then pulled out a

11

strangely shaped package wrapped in white tissue. She untaped the rustling paper. "Hey, all right . . . a conch shell!"

Her mother said, "We thought you'd like it for your shell collection."

"I sure do! Thanks!" She took the gum out of her mouth and, bringing the shell to her lips, blew mightily.

Aooooouuuuuh! it blasted. *Aooooouuuuuh!*

Grant chuckled. "It sounds like an ancient call to battle."

Her mother shot him a rueful look. "Let's hope not! I'd rather hear a call to peace . . . to a truce."

Gram took her hands from her ears. "Be sure to take that thing home with you!"

Ginger didn't care to think about taking anything *home*. That meant to the Gabriels' house now, not to the old beach house where she'd grown up. Anyhow, the beach house was already sold.

Mom glanced at Ginger's suitcase. "All ready to go?"

"I guess so," Ginger replied. She'd fought Mom and Grant falling in love; she'd even hoped to stop their wedding. What good would it do to fight now? Besides, her feelings about their marriage and moving into Grant's house were too confused, especially now that she'd become a Christian.

Gram said, "I'll miss having you here everyday, Ginger. I don't know what I'll do without you."

"I'll miss you, too, Gram." Except when she was

in school, Ginger had always stayed with Gram while Mom worked.

Gram gave her a hug. "You can always visit."

Grant put in, "And you're always welcome at our house, Mrs. Trumbell. We need a grandmother. It might seem strange to some people, but we'd like you to feel part of our family."

Strange is right, Ginger thought, ignoring how pleased her grandmother looked. Gram shouldn't like Grant Gabriel so much. After all, Mom had been married to Gram's son first!

Grant grabbed Ginger's suitcase. "We're off!"

In Grant's blue four-door Oldsmobile, her mother bubbled with excitement. "While we were gone, Ginger, I phoned the painters and told them to paint your room a light peach. And Tuesday the movers will bring our furniture, so everything will be ready before school starts."

Uff, school! Ginger thought. Just ten days away. Now she'd have to take a school bus to Santa Rosita Elementary, and she probably wouldn't know the kids on it.

Her mother turned around to the backseat. "If we can finish all of the moving and settle in, there'll be a surprise for all of us next week."

Ginger scarcely heard as she looked out the window, watching her old neighborhood pass by. The beach houses were mostly small, but this was where she'd grown up. A good thing they wouldn't be driving past her old house. She already felt sad enough.

13

As they pulled onto the freeway, her mother said, "I can't wait to see Lilabet and Joshua."

I can! Ginger thought. Lilabet, her new stepsister, was three, and Joshua, her stepbrother, was eleven. She'd begun to like them before the wedding, but now she wasn't so sure. She didn't know which was worse: moving in with them or watching Mom and Grant in the front seat. It wasn't that they sat close; it was that they seemed to belong to each other and to no one else.

At last they were at the Santa Rosita Hills off ramp. It seemed like a billion miles from the beach.

"How beautiful it is here in the countryside," Mom remarked. "Look at the lawns and flowers and trees . . . and the sunshine everywhere. No more beach fog and morning overcast."

Grant said, "I've always liked the hillsides of lemon trees. How do you like it here, Ginger?"

"It's okay," she replied, even though she preferred the beach.

After a while, Grant announced, "Here we are." It sounded as if Ginger had never been there, when she'd been coming all summer for swimming lessons and dinners, and finally the wedding reception.

They drove into a shady lane of eucalyptus trees, and there was the house. It was old, white, and Spanish—a California house that Mom called "charming." Great bursts of purple bougainvillaea bloomed against the white adobe walls, and bright red geraniums bordered the front lawn.

As they climbed from the car, Raffles, a shaggy gray-and-white blimp of a dog, hurried from the front steps. "Woof!" he barked hoarsely, wagging his entire tailless rear end at them.

"Raffles, you certainly seem glad to see us," Grant said.

The front door flew open, and Joshua ran out. "Hi, everyone!" He beamed when his father opened his arms for a hug.

"Dad-dy! Dad-dy!" Lilabet yelled as she rushed out the door, followed by Grandfather Gabriel. Her straight hair with bangs shone like a golden cap as she raced to her father.

"Here's our Lilabet!" Grant sang out, scooping her up.

After their kiss, he nodded toward Ginger's mother and asked, "And who do you think this is now?"

Lilabet's big brown eyes turned trustingly. "Mother."

"Oh, Lilabet!" Ginger's mother took the little girl into her arms. "How nice to hear you call me mother!"

Ginger stiffened. *She's not your mother*, she thought. Then she felt meaner than mean, since Lilabet's real mother was dead.

Grandfather Gabriel shook Ginger's hand. "We're so glad to have you here." He was a silvery-haired, retired minister, and she liked him a lot. "Look, Raffles is welcoming you."

Sure enough, Raffles seemed to be smiling through the long shaggy hair on his face.

"Hi, Raffles," she said, and he licked her leg. She tried to joke, "Hey, are you licking off my freckles?"

No one heard, though. Her mother was setting Lilabet down and giving Joshua a big hug.

Grant asked Grandfather Gabriel, "Did everything go well here at home?"

"Pretty well, except Lilabet seems to be catching a cold."

Lilabet grabbed Ginger's leg. "Gin-ger! Gin-ger!" she piped. She looked up at Ginger, her nose runny. "Hold me, please?"

With that runny nose? Ginger thought. Besides, she was already holding her shell. "Maybe later."

Lilabet pointed at the conch shell. "I wanna see that thing, Gin-ger. I wanna hold it."

"Maybe later," Ginger said again.

Lilabet frowned. "I wanna hold it now!"

Ginger blinked. Lilabet was usually so sweet. What had gotten into her? Ginger glanced at Joshua and found him giving her a nasty look, too.

Grandfather Gabriel said, "Please be a good girl, Lilabet." He turned to the rest of them. "I brought out the camera for a picture of your homecoming. Let's get all five of you together. . . ."

Ginger felt herself being gathered up with them to pose in front of the house. She could already imagine the picture: Mom and Grant were the back row, their arms around Joshua, Lilabet, and her.

16

"A blended family," people called it. "His kids and hers." "Ginger Trumbell and the Gabriel family. Ginger's the redhead." She tossed her gum into the nearby geraniums.

Grandfather Gabriel peered through the camera. "Smile, everyone. On the count of three . . . one, two, three."

Ginger forced a smile to her lips, and the camera clicked.

"Gin-ger, I wanna hold that," Lilabet said, pointing to the conch shell again. "I wanna hold that thing."

She'll drop it and break it into a billion pieces. "Maybe later," Ginger repeated.

"I don't like you, Gin-ger!" Lilabet yelled. She stamped a foot. "Don't come to my house . . . don't come to my house!"

"Lilabet!" Grant warned. "Even if you aren't well, that's a bad thing to say. Please tell Ginger you're sorry."

"*I'm not sorry!*" Lilabet yelled. Her face screwed up, and she began to wail.

"Lilabet, please," Grandfather Gabriel said. "Don't spoil your father's and new mother's homecoming."

Ginger cringed. It was her fault for not letting Lilabet hold the shell.

"Please, Lilabet," everyone begged, but she wailed louder.

Raffles raised his head and howled.

17

Ginger wanted to howl herself, to drown out this terrible moment. Before she knew what she was doing, she lifted the conch shell to her lips and blew. *Aooooouuuuuh . . . aooooouuuuuh . . . aooooouuuuuh . . .*

It drowned out Lilabet's wailing and Raffles' howling. And, as it floated over the neighborhood, it did sound like a call to battle. *Aooooouuuuuh . . . aooooouuuuuh!*

2

The last *aoooooouuuuuh!* hung in the summer air as Ginger took the conch shell from her lips.

Lilabet had stopped yelling, and her brown eyes were filled with awe. Mom, Grant, and Grandfather Gabriel looked ready to break into laughter, but Joshua was staring at Ginger as if he thought she were crazy.

She'd acted without thinking, she decided. She'd snapped again. "I guess it was a dumb thing to do," she said.

"Maybe not," Grant answered with a grin. "But on that memorable note, let's grab our suitcases and go in."

Lilabet said, "I wanna hold your hand, Gin-ger."

19

Ginger blinked. Had blowing the conch caused Lilabet to be friendly again? It seemed like an unfair trick. She said, "We have to take our things in now, Lilabet."

"I wanna help," her little stepsister said.

Ginger couldn't quite hide her smile. "Okay. You can help." She looked for something Lilabet could carry in. Just then the newspaper delivery truck slowed by the driveway, and the newspaper came flying. "Why don't you carry in the paper?"

"I'm getting the paper," Lilabet announced importantly to the others and ran up the driveway for it.

Grandfather observed, "Looks like you've acquired an admirer, Virginia."

"I guess so." Ginger smiled, feeling grown-up as usual when he called her Virginia. "But blowing the conch was dumb."

He laughed. "I'd say it was the high point of my day!"

She tried not to smile. "Well, I'm not going to do it again!" she vowed.

While they unloaded Grant's car, Raffles kept an eye on Ginger as if he wondered what she might do next.

"Woof!" she barked back at him. "Woof, woof!"

Smiling through his shaggy hair, he wagged his rear end.

After they'd carried the luggage and bags into the house, Grant said, "Time for your nap, Lilabet." He touched a hand to her forehead. "You do feel warmer than usual. You'll feel better after you've slept."

Lilabet frowned, then looked at Ginger.

Ginger nodded her head as if to say, *You'd better do it*.

Lilabet nodded in return. Then she followed her father down the hallway to her room. Behind them, Mom said, "I'll get out the thermometer and the baby aspirin."

Grandfather said, "Let me carry your suitcase to your room, Virginia."

My room? her mind echoed. *My room*.

He added, "Before long, you'll begin to feel at home here, even if that sounds impossible now."

She looked down at her conch shell and thought, *I hope so!*

"The neighbors—your friend Katie's mother—sent over dinner," he said. "Joshua and I thought we'd rustle up a salad to go with it. Your mother wants to do the cooking, but it doesn't seem fair that she should start the very day you arrive. By the way," he added, "you'll be sharing the bathroom with Lilabet. It's between your rooms."

Ginger wasn't sure she wanted to share anything with Lilabet after her yelling, "I don't like you, Ginger. Don't come to my house!"

"Well, here's your room," Grandfather said, setting her suitcase down. "Take your time. The Lord only expects us to live one day at a time. Sometimes only one moment at a time. Carefully . . . gingerly . . . like your name."

She had to smile. "I guess I don't do things too gingerly. Gram says I'm more like the spicy meaning of my name."

He smiled. "Well, it doesn't hurt to be spicy sometimes, too. As for that conch shell, better let me put it on the top shelf, so Lilabet can't get hold of it. She's cute, but as you've already witnessed, she can be a rascal."

Ginger handed him the conch, and he placed it on the top shelf of the white bookshelves that enclosed the window and window seat.

"There, that makes the room look more like yours already," he said. "It's just waiting for you to make your imprint."

She glanced around. The big windows over the window seat were open to the backyard, but the smell of fresh paint lingered, making her feel queasy. Painted a pale peach, the room looked different, as different as she'd felt wearing her peach junior bridesmaid dress at the wedding Saturday. White bookshelves covered the rest of the window seat wall. The twin beds' wicker headboards and the fluffy rug were white, too.

Grandfather turned to leave. "I'm very happy to be your grandfather, Virginia. I feel like we're good friends, too, since that day you accepted the Lord."

"I'm happy that you're m—my stepgrandfather, too—" Ginger replied.

"Grandfather is fine," he said.

She smiled and nodded. He was the one who'd explained to her about being a Christian on that special day at the beach. She'd known that God had sent him jogging out there to meet her. He'd warned her, too, "You won't be perfect. There'll still be a lot of the old Ginger in you."

Now Grandfather said, "I'll let you unpack and get accustomed to your room."

"Thanks," she said, and closed the door behind him.

Slowly, she began to look around. *My room*, she told herself. *My room*. The truth of it didn't want to sink in. She dug in her shorts' pocket for a stick of gum, unwrapped it, and stuck it into her mouth.

My bed, she decided about the twin bed nearest the window. After a while, she opened her suitcase on the fluffy white carpet and took out her favorite stuffed animal, Parrot. She settled him on the white chenille bedspread and announced, "We're home, Parrot. This is where we live now."

Next, she took the framed picture of her father from the suitcase and set it on the white bookshelves. "This is where I live now," she told him, too.

Finally she slid open the white shuttered closet doors and began to hang her clothes. Probably she couldn't throw her stuff around like she used to do. Probably she'd have to be disgustingly neat. She gave her gum a loud crack.

She'd just put everything away when someone knocked. "It's me," her mother said. "May I come in?"

"Sure," Ginger said, opening the door.

Mom's blue eyes sparkled. "Hi. I just wanted to see if you're getting settled." She came in and closed the door behind her, then looked around the room. "Well, you're doing wonderfully." Her gaze stopped at the picture of Ginger's father before moving on.

"I'm all unpacked," Ginger offered.

"Good." Mom smiled encouragingly. "I'm so grateful you've accepted this change in our lives, Ginger. I know it's not easy for you. It's strange for me here, too."

"It is?"

Her mother nodded. "I'm sure it's strange for all of us, but we'll get used to it. We'll be happy; you'll see."

Ginger hoped so. If only Mom didn't belong to Grant and all of the rest of them, too. For three whole years, there'd been just the two of them.

"Well, I'd better get busy while Lilabet's sleeping," Mom said. "Please be quiet if you use the bathroom. Let's hope she feels better when she wakes up." She smiled. "I never dreamed that conch shell would be so useful!"

Ginger had to grin herself.

When her mother left, Ginger brushed her wild red curls. It didn't do much good, but she hoped she looked good enough for the Gabriels.

When she'd finished, she made her way through the house. Everything seemed different, maybe because the painters were gone and the wedding gifts put away. Most of the walls were a creamy white, and the furniture was dark wood—antiques Grant had inherited from his mother's family. There were angels all over too: carved wooden ones; crystal, straw, and metal angels; even paintings of angels; and angel trivets on the dining room wall. Grant said his mother had begun to collect them when she married Grandfather Gabriel. "Anyone with a name like Gabriel has to have an angel collection," she'd said.

After a while, Ginger stepped outside. The backyard was big, and flowers bloomed around the lawn. She wondered if Grandfather Gabriel had gotten settled in the guest house behind the swimming pool last week. He and Grant had moved into the house with Lilabet and Joshua two years ago, after Grant's first wife and Grandfather's wife died in the freeway accident.

Ginger almost didn't see Joshua. He sat on the red-tiled bench near the ping-pong table, leaning back against the house. He grumbled, "Dad said I should ask you to play ping-pong."

She ignored his tone. "Okay. You been practicing?"

He put down the table's backboard. "A little."

"Yeah, I bet." Anyhow, it didn't matter, because she'd practiced every day at Gram's house last week.

She grabbed a paddle. She'd win, she told herself. And she'd beat this awful feeling of being an outsider, too.

"Rally for serve?" Joshua asked.

"Sure." He was right-handed, so when he bounced the ball to her side of the table, she slammed it back to his left.

To her amazement, he slammed it to her left side, and she barely returned it. "Hey, you have been practicing!"

He grinned a little and missed the ball.

She served first, giving the ball so much spin that his paddle fanned air. Her second serve slammed to his left corner so fast he missed it, too.

She beat him all three games, but barely. "You're getting good!" she said, collapsing on the nearby red-tiled bench.

"Not good enough to beat you yet, but I will," he answered. He raised a side of the ping-pong table into practice position and began to hit the ball against it.

At the Santa Rosita fair, when she'd asked him to help stop the wedding, Joshua had said he liked Mom a lot and that their parents getting married wouldn't ruin things. So what was wrong with him now?

Before long, they had to set the patio table, and he didn't act any friendlier. Worst of all, at dinner she had to sit between him and Mom, and they all held hands around the table as they sang grace.

After their "Amen," Lilabet sat smiling at her

from across the table. "Green fingernails!" she piped. "Gin-ger's got green fingernails again!"

Everyone smiled a little, and Ginger tried to hide her hands. They probably all thought she was a bad example for Lilabet. Why, oh, why did she always do dumb things?

"Wasn't it lovely of Katie's mother to send over the lasagna tonight?" Ginger's mother asked. "Here, let me get the foil off the casserole." As she did, the wonderful cheese and tomato aroma of lasagna filled the air.

Grant said, "Ummm, smells good." He began to slice the lasagna. "Katie's parents are already fine neighbors. I'm so glad Ginger will have a girl her age living nearby."

"Too bad Katie and Ginger will be attending different schools," Grandfather remarked.

"We've been giving that some thought," Grant replied.

"Grant—" her mother warned, then quickly added, "could you serve Lilabet, please?"

Uh-oh, Ginger thought. She felt sure Mom was nudging Grant with her foot under the table. What did Grant mean, they were giving that some thought? Did they want her to go to Santa Rosita Christian, too? She'd have asked, but her mother was already talking about how lovely the peach-colored paint had turned out in Ginger's room.

"Won't it look wonderful when the movers bring the rest of your things for the shelves, Ginger?" her mother continued. "Your shell collection and stuffed animals and the rest?"

"I guess so," Ginger replied, worried. Just then the salad bowl reached her, so she didn't have to face them.

"By the way," Mom added, "we have to get up early tomorrow to finish cleaning out the beach house. Grant and Joshua are going to help us with the yard sale in the afternoon. Your father said he'd come to get his things."

Ginger spilled lettuce over the edge of her plate. "Dad's going to be there?" she asked.

"Yes, of course," Mom answered. "He has old surfboards and other belongings stored in the garage."

Ginger realized all of them were watching her.

Grant passed her a plate of lasagna and said, "It's a little strange now for all of us, Ginger, but we'll work matters out. We're going to have a good family life together."

She nodded, not so sure. Maybe if things didn't work out, she and Mom could move away. Mom could get another divorce. Some people got divorced five or six times.

"God is already working it out," her mother said. Then she looked at Grant so lovingly that Ginger knew there'd be no chance of moving, not yet anyhow.

God, please help me work things out, too, she prayed. *It's so strange to be moving here. It's so strange for my life to be changing so much.*

It seemed to her that God answered in a still, small voice, using Grandfather Gabriel's word: *gingerly . . . gingerly.*

That meant carefully. Grandfather had said she should always be "holding the Lord's hand." She wasn't sure what that meant, but she guessed she'd find out.

3

Through the grayness of sleep, Ginger thought she heard knocking. "Who's there?" she mumbled into her pillow.

"Wake up, Ginger," her mother said.

Ginger opened her eyes and saw the pale peach walls. The Gabriel house . . . or was she dreaming? No, there were Parrot, Dad's picture, the conch shell, and her other things on the bookshelves.

"Breakfast's almost ready," her mother said. "Please don't go back to sleep."

It seemed to Ginger there was something she didn't want to face. She sat up groggily. "Who, me?"

Her mother smiled. "Yes, you. Be sure to wear

your grubbies. It's going to be a busy day, cleaning up our old house and having the yard sale this afternoon."

That's what she didn't want to face, Ginger remembered: her old house . . . her room . . . her father.

"When you're awake, Ginger, there's something important I'd like to discuss with you," her mother said. Just then the oven timer began to buzz down the hallway. "We'll talk later."

The smell of baking muffins spurred Ginger on. She started for the bathroom she shared with Lilabet. Last night, she'd nearly fallen over Lilibet's plastic stepstool, and the tub had held a jumble of plastic ducks, frogs, boats, and spongy blocks.

This morning Lilabet, who wore a pink nightie, stood on the stepstool by the sink. "Gin-ger!" she piped. Her mouth and chin were foamy with toothpaste. "I brush my teeth!"

"So I see," Ginger said. "Guess I'll get dressed while you're in here." It was going to take some getting used to living with Lilabet—and everyone else.

When Ginger arrived at the breakfast table, Mom, Grant, and Joshua were already eating. Nearby, Lilabet sat in her booster chair picking blueberries from a muffin. "Where's Grandfather Gabriel?" Ginger asked.

"He has a small kitchen in the guest house," Grant explained. "He plans to do most of his own cooking there for himself."

"Oh . . . I didn't know that." She sat down and sipped her orange juice. She felt a little guilty. Was it Mom's and her fault that he'd moved out of the house?

"One of the reasons we bought this place was the guest house," Grant said. "He'd always planned to move there someday. He loves us dearly, but he could use a little more quiet in his life. He plans to do some writing."

Her mother remarked, "I'm afraid he won't start his writing today. Not with taking Joshua shopping for school clothes. I'm grateful he's taking Lilabet with them so we can get more accomplished."

Over his cereal Joshua said sleepily, "I hate shopping."

"So do a lot of us," Grant replied, "but that doesn't help. The best thing to do when unpleasant matters lie ahead is to ask the Lord to help. You might end up enjoying what you've been dreading."

Ginger bit into a blueberry muffin. She didn't like shopping very much either, but she almost wished she were going with them. Strange that she'd wanted so badly to see her father all summer . . . and now she hoped he wouldn't show up.

They drove from the sunshine in Santa Rosita Hills into a gray overcast sky by the beach. Ginger felt jammed into the backseat, almost buried in empty boxes and suitcases. She was glad when Grant parked in front of the old two-bedroom stucco house, under Ginger's favorite palm tree.

"Time to get to work," her mother said as they climbed out of the car.

No sign of Dad, Ginger noted. But it was still early and Saturday morning. He was probably out surfing.

Grant said, "I'll get the moving cartons from the trunk." He wore grubby jeans and looked eager to help. "Can the two of you carry in the empty suitcases?"

"Sure," Ginger answered. She wondered if the neighbors realized they were moving, not that it was unusual or mattered much. People moved in or out nearly every month by the beach.

Starting up the sidewalk with two big suitcases, she looked at the house she'd lived in all of her life. How small it was. Hadn't she ever really seen it before?

Inside, the house was familiar, yet strange, too. She and Mom had only been gone one week, but the house no longer felt quite like it belonged to them.

"I'll tape up the cartons," Grant offered.

Ginger's mother set down the suitcases she'd borrowed from Grant and looked over her clipboard of lists. "I still have to make decisions about what to sell and what to take with us."

Ginger eyed the living room furniture. Most of it was comfortable but beat-up. They'd bought lots of it at yard sales. She remembered her father saying, "I don't want you buying used stuff. When we buy

something, I want it to be first class. No more junk."
But Mom had said she'd rather have secondhand
things than nothing.

Ginger said, "I guess Dad wouldn't want any of
it."

Her mother glanced up from her clipboard. "I
phoned him last night, and he only wants his
belongings from the garage. His apartment doesn't
have much storage space."

"Oh," Ginger said.

"Could you finish packing the things in your
room?" her mother asked. "The more we pack
ourselves, the less we'll have to pay the movers.
Take two suitcases and some cartons."

"Okay." Ginger grabbed the empty suitcases and
carried them to what Mom always called her
"brown cave of a room." Even it looked different
now—dark and dingy. She pulled open the drapes,
and that helped a little. Still, her bed and maple
desk and chair seemed dingy, too. She opened her
closet. It was full of junk, even though she'd already
cleaned out lots of it before the wedding. Maybe
she'd throw away some more.

By eleven o'clock Ginger had filled the suitcases
with clothes, and the cartons with her stuffed animal collection and other belongings. In the kitchen,
Grant was still packing plates and cups from the
shelves. Mom had packed up everything else, and
now she walked around checking items off her list.

"Ginger," she said, "if you'd get started in the

garage, it'd be a help. Yard sale things are marked with green tape."

"Okay," Ginger agreed, feeling uneasy. She shoved another stick of gum into her mouth.

Outside, she unlocked the garage. She'd just started piling flowerpots and junk into her battered old wagon when she heard a car pull up. Chewing her gum fast and hard, she glanced out the garage door.

To her surprise, her father got out of a pickup truck.

The sight of him riveted her to the garage floor. His kinky dark curls were damp, probably from surfing. He wore white shorts and a white T-shirt and, as usual, he looked like a prince, a real prince; he was that handsome.

His eyes found her, and a smile flashed beneath his thick, dark moustache. "Hi there, kiddo," he said.

Her voice sounded weird. "Hi."

"I see you're still wearing green fingernails," he remarked.

She smiled and remembered to chew her gum again.

He raised a dark brow at her, then eyed the old one-car garage. "Looks like you've cleaned up a little in here."

"We did some of it before the wedding," she answered, and then turned red. Why did she have to go and mention the word "wedding"?

"You having a yard sale?" he asked.

"This afternoon. Didn't Mom tell you on the phone?"

"I can't remember. Maybe she did."

Ginger couldn't take her eyes from him. She felt a jumble of confused feelings. She loved him, she really did, but—

"Something wrong?" he asked.

"The house and my room and everything seem different today," she said. "Maybe I thought you'd be different, too."

He laughed. "You're crazy. I'm the same as ever, kiddo. I don't ever plan to change." He tousled her hair, then gave the top of her head a hard knuckle rub. "Hey, kiddo, you mad at me or something?"

She pulled away. "Not anymore, I guess. Dad, I—"

"Hey, what's this 'Dad' stuff?" he asked. "Remember me? I'm Steve. Save the Dad stuff for Grant Gabriel. It makes me sound like an old man."

"I'm sorry," Ginger managed.

He turned away, looking at the yard. After a while he said lightly, "Lucky I got here before all my stuff was sold."

She guessed he was trying to change the subject. "You know Mom and I wouldn't sell your old surfboards and stuff."

"You wouldn't?" he asked.

"No. It makes me feel awful, you saying that."

He grinned. "That so?"

She smiled a little. "Yeah, that's so."

"Anyhow," he said, "I borrowed a pickup to haul my stuff to Gram's." He opened a big cardboard carton and poked around in it. "When are you moving in with the lovebirds?"

She gave her gum a loud crack. Gram had told him on the phone, but Ginger decided to tell him again. "I moved in with Mom and Grant yesterday afternoon. I'm living there now."

"Oh."

She hoped he'd say "Good luck" or something, but he started whistling instead and repacking his stuff.

Ginger said, "Gram told me maybe you were going to move to Hawaii and get married."

"It didn't work out," he answered, not looking at her.

After a while she suggested, "Maybe you could visit Gram more. She feels sad about Mom and me moving across town."

He shouldered the carton. "You're beginning to sound as bossy as your mother," he said. He started down the driveway.

"Mom's not bossy," Ginger said in a calm voice.

"Now that's news!" he laughed. "And I've got news for you. You're going to hate living away from the beach. This is where everything's happening."

Something kept her from snapping again. What was wrong with him anyhow? Was he just jealous about Mom remarrying? He sure hadn't cared this summer. When she'd tried to get him to stop the romance, he'd said, "We've been divorced for three years now. What she does is her own business." Then he'd said, "Hang tough, kiddo."

Ginger pulled the wagon to the front yard and unloaded flowerpots and other sale junk. Darting a glance toward the front door, she hoped Mom and Grant would stay inside.

When she returned to the garage, her father said, "You know, something seems different about you. You're not snapping like you used to."

She brightened. "It's because I'm a Christian now."

His lips parted. "Not you, too!"

"I've been one for about two weeks! I'm even going to be baptized at church next month."

"Baptized?!" He stared at her, then finally shook his head. "Well, you'll probably get over it."

"I don't want to get over it!" she said. "I've got joy in my heart now . . . usually anyhow." She'd had almost two joyful weeks until being uprooted from Gram's house.

Her father said, "Well, with your mother claiming to be a Christian, you probably had to give in to keep the peace." He ran a hand through his curls again. "On top of which she marries the principal of a Christian school!"

"But that's not why I'm a Christian. If only—"

"Don't you start in on me!" he protested. "I'm happy just the way I am."

38

She said quietly, "You don't act happy."

His face hardened and he headed away with the wagon.

When he came back up the driveway, she heard the front screen door slam. Out came Mom and Grant, carrying boxes for the yard sale. Ginger glanced back at her father. Judging from his wary look, he realized they were there, too.

Her mother's voice sounded slightly strangled as she called out, "Hi, Steve!"

"Hi," he replied, looking tense.

Mom's brownish-red hair gleamed in the sunlight, and her dimples deepened. She looked so beautiful, even in her jeans and blue T-shirt, Ginger was sure he'd be sorry about the divorce. Mom added, "I'm glad you could make it. I didn't know what you'd want done with your things."

"I'll get them out of your way in no time," Dad replied.

"Thanks." Mom hesitated, then said, "Steve, I'd like you to meet Grant Gabriel."

Grant stepped forward and reached out his big hand. "It's nice to meet you."

Her father said, "Well, why not?"

To Ginger's amazement, they were shaking hands. She didn't know what she'd expected, but she hadn't expected that!

Grant asked, "Need any help carrying things to the truck?"

"No thanks," Dad answered stiffly. "I'm about

done. Just the old surfboards and stuff. If you'll excuse me, I'll finish loading up."

"Sure," Grant replied.

He and Mom wandered over to the lawn, puttering with things they'd brought out for the yard sale. They took forever poking through the boxes. A crazy idea formed in Ginger's mind. Did they think Dad—Steve—would try to kidnap her? Ha, no chance! Maybe some fathers did that, but he didn't even like to be with her!

"Well, time to go," her father said. He gave her head another hard knuckle rub. "By the way, I don't like the idea of your going to Santa Rosita Christian."

"But I'm not!" she protested, pulling away. "I'm going to my old school."

"Oh, yeah?" he asked. "That's not what I hear."

She could see he was serious. Mom had wanted to discuss something "important" with her this morning . . . and last night Grant mentioned her being in school with Katie.

Her father raised a dark eyebrow. "Why don't you ask your mom what she said last night when she called?"

"She told you last night?"

His brown eyes glittered. "Maybe my opinion no longer counts, but I'm going to tell you what I think before I go. I say you'd better forget this religious stuff and toughen up again, kiddo. Toughen up, or you'll really be miserable."

40

He turned abruptly, and Ginger watched him all the way to the truck and even as he drove away.

Suddenly Mom was there, putting an arm around Ginger's shoulder. "What's wrong? Did he say something to upset you?"

Ginger hesitated; then she blurted, "He said you're sending me to Santa Rosita Christian!"

"Oh, Ginger, that's what I've wanted to discuss with you, but we've been so busy. It's not the way he made it sound. We've only talked about it. There's been no decision."

"Your mother and I discussed it on our trip," Grant said. "You know, Joshua goes to school there, and your friend, Katie, and someday Lilabet will, too."

Ginger protested, "I've always gone to Santa Rosita Elementary . . . always."

"We know, dear," her mother said. "And you've had so many other changes this year that we want you to decide."

"That's easy. I want to go to my old school!"

Grant said, "Let's give it some time, Ginger. We want God's will to be done in this matter, not ours. God knows what's best for your future. If you'll turn it over to Him, He'll let you know what to do."

Ginger turned away, remembering Dad's words: *Toughen up again or you'll really be miserable.*

She was sure Mom and Grant wanted her to go to Santa Rosita Christian—yet, if she did, her father would be furious. Either way, she couldn't win.

4

As she stood in front of her old house, Ginger's mind reeled. Her thoughts went from her father's "Forget that religious stuff" to Grant's "God will show you what to do." She clenched her fists. She didn't want to change schools, but what if God wanted her at Santa Rosita Christian?

A woman came up the sidewalk and asked, "Has your yard sale started yet?"

"Not quite," Ginger's mother said, "but come see what's already out. There's furniture inside for sale, too." She led the woman to the flowerpots and boxes of bric-a-brac.

Grant called over, "I'll get the rest out in a minute." He turned to Ginger. "I hope you'll take a few days to decide about school. Even a week if you need it."

Ginger swallowed hard. "How will I know what God wants me to do?"

"You'll know in your heart when He tells you," Grant promised. "Do you want me to pray for you?"

"I guess so." To her surprise, Grant took her hands in his and closed his eyes to pray right there in the front yard.

"Dear Heavenly Father," he began. "You are the creator of the universe, of planets and stars, of this earth and its great oceans. You also caused Ginger Trumbell to be created. Thank You for letting her begin to know You through Your Son, Jesus Christ. Father, she needs to know where You want her to go to school. We pray for Your clear answer to this in Christ's name, and we thank You in advance. Amen."

He opened his eyes and smiled at her kindly.

What will God do? she wondered.

"We'd better give your mother a hand," Grant said.

Before long, the front lawn was covered with old pictures, draperies, books, ladders, her old toys, and furniture. Cars pulled up, and more and more people came to rummage through everything. They bought piles of stuff, even beat-up toys, old clothes, and musty books.

Mom sat at the card table, smiling up at people

and making change from the money box. She'd say, "I hope you'll enjoy this," or "I hope you get good use from it."

Ginger helped carry shoppers' purchases to their cars and trucks, trying to forget her school problem.

At one o'clock Lilabet and Joshua arrived with Grandfather Gabriel. "My land, what a thriving business!" he said. "It's a good thing we brought you hamburgers and milk shakes to keep up your strength."

"A good thing is right," Grant said. "We could use Joshua to stay and help, too . . . if you're willing, Josh."

"If I have to," Joshua grumbled.

His father warned, "I don't like that tone, Josh. You don't have to help if you don't care to."

Joshua looked down at the grass. "I'll help."

Ginger didn't want him to help sell her old stuff, but what could she do about it?

Lilabet had been hanging onto Grandfather's legs, and now she piped, "Horse!" She raced over to climb on Ginger's old battered rocking horse, then rocked wildly and whooped.

Grant hurried to her. "Looks like I might have to buy your old rocking horse, Ginger."

"She can have it," Ginger said. "It could be my present."

"That's mighty generous of you," he called back. "I'll take it up with your mother."

Grandfather opened a bag and handed Ginger a

beautifully wrapped package. "A present for you."

"Really? For me?"

"Yes, for you." His gray-blue eyes twinkled. "Open it."

She ripped off the flowery paper, then opened the box. A Bible. A cream-colored Bible with a picture of Jesus joyously holding a lamb, surrounded by happy kids.

"Open it to the first page," he urged.

Presented to Virginia Anne Trumbell by Matthew Grant Gabriel, it said.

Grandfather said, "Sounds pretty formal, doesn't it? Maybe I should have written 'To Ginger from Grandfather.' "

"It sounds just right to me," she said. "Thanks. Thanks a lot." She looked up at him. "Grant says sometimes God speaks through the Bible."

"Indeed He does," Grandfather agreed. "Very often."

"It's funny you'd give it to me right now," she said. "I need Him to tell me something."

"Nothing funny about it," he answered with a smile. "When you believe in God, your life is full of what other people often call amazing coincidences."

She smiled up at him, then gazed at the picture of Jesus on the Bible. "Do you think He really looked like that?"

Grandfather studied it with her. "No one really knows, but I like to think of Him as a strong carpenter. In those days, a carpenter didn't have ready-cut wood. He'd chop down the trees, haul them to his shop, and saw and plane them by hand. I see Jesus as strong with big shoulders, and filled with goodness."

Her mother called over, "Ginger, can you help here?"

"I'll take your Bible back home with me if you like," Grandfather said. "I'm taking Lilabet back for her nap. She's a little old for the rocking horse, but she certainly looks fond of it. Wonder if it'll fit in my trunk."

By five o'clock, the yard sale was over. Ginger's mother said, "I didn't dream we'd sell most of these things."

Grant asked, "What's that old saying? 'One person's junk is another's treasure'?"

"It must be!" Mom laughed.

As they drove home in the car, Grant asked her, "Should we tell Ginger and Joshua about the surprise?"

"Let's," Mom said. "You tell them."

Ginger glanced aside at Joshua, but he seemed curious, too. She hoped it wouldn't be another awful surprise like this morning's, about maybe changing schools.

Grant told them as he drove, "We have a lot to accomplish before school starts, but things are going well so far. If we get the rest of the moving done and the house organized, we thought we might all go to Disneyland next week and stay over one night. Each of you could take a friend."

"All right!" Joshua said. "I'll ask Mike Morgan."

"All right!" Ginger echoed. Then she remembered that her best friend, Mandy, had moved away. "Who could I ask?"

"How about Katie Cameron?" Mom suggested. "She's new here. I'm sure she's never been to Disneyland."

"Yeah, I guess I could ask her," Ginger decided.

Grant warned, "Now don't get too excited about it yet. We still have to get everything done, and I go back to work full-time next week. The movers will bring what's left in the beach house Tuesday, and we'll want to get it all put away. That means shovels, rakes, and tools in the garage, Josh, and helping move things around the house. And, Ginger, that means putting away your things and helping your mother all you can."

"I'll get my part done!" Ginger promised. She hadn't been to Disneyland for years. The thought of going next week was so exciting that she forgot about school.

Even Joshua was excited and promised to do his part.

At bedtime, Ginger thumbed through her Bible. Scattered through it were pictures: *The Creation, Noah's Ark, Joseph and His Brothers in Egypt, Moses Receives the Ten Commandments, Jesus Is Born.* What a lot she had to learn.

When she finally closed her eyes, she prayed, *God, where do You want me to go to school?* She listened for a long time, but He didn't say a thing.

The next day was Sunday, and they picked up Gram on the way to church. "How nice to have you going with us," Ginger's mother said as Gram climbed into the backseat beside Ginger.

Gram's brown eyes sparkled. "I went when I was a girl, but that's a long time ago." She winked at Ginger. "I figure if it's done you so much good, it might make a difference in me, too."

Embarrassed, Ginger smoothed her green flowered dress. "I'm still not so good," she admitted.

"Not perfect," Gram said, "but you're better."

Ginger wondered what Dad—Steve—would think about Gram coming to church with them. *Forget about that religious stuff. Toughen up again, kiddo, or you'll be miserable,* he'd said.

Sunday school hadn't begun when Ginger arrived in her room. "Katie!" Ginger said. "Wait till I tell you what we're going to do!"

Katie hurried through the crowd of kids to Ginger. Her straight brown hair was tied into her usual ponytail, and her brown eyes were warm with friendship. She asked in her soft southern voice, "What are we going to do?"

"*If* my family gets all of the moving and unpacking done, we get to go to Disneyland this week— and you can come with us!"

"You're teasing!" Katie exclaimed.

"No, really and truly," Ginger promised. "Mom said she'd talk to your mother about it today."

"I surely would like to go," Katie said, except her *I* sounded like *Ah*. The more excited she got, the more southern she talked. "I could help you with your room. Is everything moved in?"

"Just clothes I brought from Gram's in my suitcase. And the stuff we brought home in the car after the yard sale."

Katie said, "I'll help tomorrow if you'd like."

"Sure," Ginger answered.

Their Sunday school teacher, Mrs. Tyler, stood up front and smiled like sunshine. "Welcome, everyone. Shall we start with 'This Is the Day'?"

Ginger knew most of the words now and sang out, "This is the day that the Lord has made. . . ." Everyone seemed joyous as they sang about "being glad in it." Next they sang, "We are one in the Spirit, we are one in the Lord. . . ." If only she'd known before how special Sunday school could be.

After roll call and announcements, Mrs. Tyler showed them their memory verse on the blackboard. *Put on the new self, created to be like God in true righteousness and holiness. Ephesians 4:24.*

Mrs. Tyler asked, "Who knows what that means?"

Katie raised her hand. "When we become Christians, we are different people."

"Very good, Katie. New Christians are new people, new selves," Mrs. Tyler replied. "We are to be

49

holy and good, and we do that by staying close to Jesus. We let Him be our Lord."

Like what was happening to her, Ginger thought as they copied the verse on a card to take home. Sometimes she still felt as snappish as the old Ginger, but when she remembered about God, she felt joyous. Other people—like Gram and even Dad—said she was better, so she must be, even if she didn't always think so herself.

Mrs. Tyler said, "The Christian life is a great change from the life a person has before coming to know Jesus. Life becomes an exciting adventure. We're going to study about what happened to a man named Paul when he became a Christian."

Listening to the lesson, Ginger marveled that such a terrible man—one who had helped kill Christians—turned into a great Christian himself. What would happen to her now that she was one?

Mrs. Tyler read from the Bible that they were to stop lying, stealing, and being angry. "We're to be tenderhearted and forgiving, just as God has forgiven us because we belong to Christ."

Before long they were singing their closing song, "God Is So Good." Ginger still felt a little shy about Sunday school, but she liked it.

When she returned home, she found Ephesians 4:24 in her new Bible. It said the very same thing she had copied on her card. She stuck the memory verse card against Parrot on the bookshelf. It looked like he was saying, "Put on the new self."

5

The next day, Labor Day, Katie arrived mid-morning. "I'm ready to labor!" she announced.

"There's lots to do," Ginger said. "Grant brought another load of my stuff. Come on, my room's a mess."

In Ginger's room, Katie looked at the clothes piled on the twin beds. "It looks like my room when we moved in. What should I do first?"

"What would you like to do?"

"Hang clothes," Katie answered. "I like to fix up closets and things."

"You do?" Ginger marveled, scarcely believing anyone would like that kind of work. "Well, good. Then I'll unpack my other junk."

Katie picked up one of Ginger's rumpled sweaters and folded it. "How's that?"

"Perfect," Ginger answered. "You have more patience than I do with folding things. I don't think that even being a Christian will make me neat."

Katie laughed, and Ginger had to grin herself.

"Maybe I'll start with my seashells," she said. As she began to unpack them, she realized how dirty they were. "I'd better wash them, whether I want to or not!"

She carried the boxes to the bathroom and turned on the tub water. They'd have to share the bathtub with Lilabet's tub toys. She'd barely gotten started when Lilabet's doorknob turned.

Lilabet peered into the bathroom. "Hi, Gin-ger."

"Hi. I thought you were supposed to play in your room."

Ignoring her words, Lilabet edged in and eyed the shells. "Can I hold 'em?"

"Not now," Ginger said.

"Please?" Lilabet begged. "Only one minute? Please, Gin-ger?"

Raffles nosed in behind her, curious.

"Just this one," Ginger said. "I'll put it by your ear so you can hear. It sounds like the ocean."

Lilabet listened wide-eyed, then grabbed the shell and held it to Raffles' ear.

Raffles woofed.

"I wanna hear more," Lilabet said.

"No, Lilabet. We're trying to get things done so we can go to Disneyland."

"Please, Gin-ger?"

Ginger handed her two more shells, but that wasn't enough either. Getting impatient, Ginger said, "If you have to hear all of them, we'll never get to Disneyland!"

Lilabet screwed up her face. "I wanna! I'll tell! I'll tell Daddy!" She ran out of the room and wailed piteously.

Raffles followed Lilabet down the hallway, howling with her.

Ginger froze, sure there'd be trouble. Suddenly she knew what to do. She raced into her room for the conch shell and getting it down, she grabbed a deep breath and blew. *Aooooouuuuuh!* it blasted, resounding through the room.

Wide-eyed, Katie asked, "Ginger, what *are* you doing?"

Ginger smiled conspiratorially. "Listen."

Before long, Lilabet peeked around the corner, teary-eyed. "I'll be nice," she promised. "I'm going to my room." She hurried off and closed the door behind her.

Katie's brown eyes danced. "Can I borrow that conch when my brothers are driving me crazy?"

Ginger laughed. "Sure." She was surprised that no one came running. "Everyone must be outside," she decided. "Or maybe they guessed what the trouble was about and didn't want any part of it."

"It must feel strange to move in with a new family," Katie said, folding a sweatshirt.

"It sure does."

"That must be your daddy's picture on the bookshelf," Katie said. "I noticed it before."

Ginger nodded.

"He surely is handsome," Katie added.

"Yeah," Ginger said. "I guess he is." For some reason, that no longer struck her as too important.

"It's strange to move far away, too," Katie said. "Georgia seems like the other side of the earth from here."

"I guess that would take getting used to, too." Ginger climbed up the bookshelf and put the conch back on the top shelf, out of Lilabet's reach.

"I prayed to have a special friend here," Katie said.

"You did?"

Katie nodded, and they smiled at each other. It felt good to have a friend.

Katie had to go home for lunch, but in the afternoon she helped again, hanging clothes in the closet and folding others, which she piled neatly in a corner to await delivery of Ginger's chest of drawers.

Ginger was tempted to tell Katie about asking God where she should attend school. And to tell her, too, that she couldn't stand one more change, even if it meant going to the best school in the world. Only Katie would probably want her to go to Santa Rosita Christian.

By dinnertime, the suitcases and boxes were empty and put away. Everything was neatly in place. Ginger said, "It *is* beginning to look like my room, even if I'm not usually this neat."

"You did a neat job on your shelves," Katie pointed out. She adjusted the shutters over the window seat until their openings matched, then fussed with the white swagged draperies.

Ginger chewed her gum and surveyed the room. The shelves around the window and window seat looked amazingly neat, and her seashells sparkled. Books stood upright, separated by driftwood, rocks, and her globe. The games were stacked. The colorful dolls from around the world that Mom's parents, Nana and Grandpa Allan, sent from Virginia were finally on display. But what made it look most homelike was her stuffed animal collection: Spider, Octopus, Dinosaur, Fish, Fair Lion, and Parrot, who still held the Bible verse card that said, "Put on the new self."

She'd truly been trying to "put on the new self," even if she had blown the conch at Lilabet. What she wanted from God in exchange was for Him to tell her loudly, "Ginger, go back to Santa Rosita Elementary."

Tuesday morning over breakfast, Ginger, Joshua, and Lilabet bid Grant good-bye as he left for work.

"Be sure to help Mom," Grant asked all of them. "I'm sorry I can't be with her and the movers."

Ginger's mother said, "I'll go out with you, Grant," and he smiled broadly at her.

Kissing, Ginger guessed, not that she cared so much anymore. She glanced across the table at Joshua and wondered if he cared at all. He was eating cereal smothered with strawberries, banana slices, and raisins as if nothing else mattered. She asked, "Don't you mind your father calling Mom 'Mom' when she isn't yours?"

Joshua shrugged. "She said I could call her Sallie or Mom or Mother, if I wanted. I'm not going to make a big deal of it. Maybe I won't call her anything."

"I call your dad Grant," Ginger pointed out.

"That's different. Your dad's still alive."

"Yeah." She didn't want to get started on that. Instead, she blurted, "It must have been awful when your mother died."

Joshua's spoon stopped halfway to his mouth, and he held it there for a tense second.

She said quickly, "At least you're used to having a sister around. I'm used to being an only child."

He narrowed his eyes. "You act like it sometimes, too."

She shot him a nasty look. "That's not nice."

His eyes darted meaningfully toward Lilabet, who was watching and listening to every word from her booster chair.

Dumb, dumb, dumb, dumb, Ginger told herself. "I guess I shouldn't have mentioned that."

"Never mind," he said, which made Ginger feel even worse.

After a while, Mom returned to the kitchen, humming happily, which didn't cheer Ginger much.

"The movers will be at the beach house at nine," Mom said. "We'd better leave in a few minutes, Ginger. Joshua's staying here with Lilabet." She turned to him. "I really appreciate your helping, Joshua. If we all work together as a family, we'll make it to Disneyland this week yet."

On the ride to the beach house, Mom called out items for Ginger to write on a grocery list. She'd say, "Tomatoes, lettuce, and celery," then she'd think aloud, "Wonder if there's sherbet for dessert?" and "Where did I put that recipe?" and "We'll have to do something right away about school clothes."

Why'd she have to mention school clothes? Ginger grumbled to herself. If only she didn't have to go to school at all. Worst of all, and despite all of her prayers, God hadn't spoken a word to her about school. *God,* she prayed again, *where do You want me to go?*

Maybe if He didn't answer, that meant she should stay at Santa Rosita Elementary. This summer had been bad enough with the wedding and moving in with the Gabriels. Who needed to be a new kid at a new school? And who knew what they'd do at a Christian school? Maybe they'd expect her to know all kinds of things and to be . . . holy!

The movers arrived late at the beach house.

When Mom suggested anything, they'd say, "We know what we're doin', lady." It took forever for them to pack the lamps and other stuff, then to carry the furniture and boxes out to their truck.

It was one o'clock before Ginger and Mom drove back to the Gabriel house, the moving truck behind them. When they arrived, the movers said, "We get an hour for lunch." They didn't finish unloading until dinnertime.

After the movers left, Ginger gazed hopelessly at the mess. Boxes of linens crowded bathrooms and hallways; furniture, lamps, plants, and pictures were scattered everywhere. Her own bedroom held three huge boxes, not to mention her maple chest of drawers and scarred desk and chair. Cardboard cartons of dishes, pots and pans, and other stuff jammed the kitchen.

Her mother said, "I'll have to manage dinner somehow."

Outside, Joshua was grouchily putting away yard tools, buckets, paint cans, ladders, garbage cans, and other junk.

Grant came home, stepping into the kitchen where Ginger unpacked cans of food onto the pantry shelves, and Mom made salad by the sink. He echoed Ginger's reaction: "What a mess!"

Mom laughed and asked him, "How were things at school?"

"About like this, but it's always hectic the week before school starts. Late textbook deliveries, last-minute applications from new students. . . ."

New students . . . He said that to get me to go there, Ginger thought.

Mom's cheeks dimpled coyly and she teased, "A bad time for us to have gotten married?"

"Now that I see you here, I don't think so." He must have forgotten Ginger, because he grabbed Mom for a kiss.

Ginger cleared her throat with a loud "Hurrummmph" and accidently knocked over a stack of cans in the pantry.

Wednesday morning, Joshua had to clean the pool and do yard work. He was grouchier yet since his friend, Mike, couldn't go to Disneyland after all. Ginger, Mom, and Lilabet went to the beach house to vacuum, wash windows, and clean.

Strange as the beach house had seemed to Ginger on Saturday, it felt even stranger to see it empty. Standing in her bedroom, Ginger sadly thought, *Good-bye.* She wandered from room to room.

"Learn from the past," Grandfather Gabriel had told her, "then put it behind you." But could she? Could she put her past behind her?

It took all day to clean the beach house, but finally everything sparkled.

Thursday, as they unpacked more boxes, Ginger prayed more anxiously, *God, where do You want me to go to school?*

He didn't answer, and Mom and Grant didn't

ask, but she bet they were praying about it, too.

The best thing they did all week, Ginger thought, was to swim in the pool every night before they went to bed. She could float on her back now, and she liked to lie in the warm, silky water and gaze up into the dark night sky. From in the pool, Grant would point up and say, "There's the Milky Way, and there's the Big Dipper and the Little Dipper." He knew all about stars and planets and the whole universe. When everyone quieted, night birds hooted and twittered, and sometimes coyotes wailed far away in the darkness.

The other thing Ginger liked was Grant giving a short Bible study before dinner. He'd read a few verses from the Bible, like about loving God with all of your heart, soul, and mind. Then they'd all discuss what it meant to them. Just talking about God made them feel more like a family.

What she liked least, besides Joshua's grouchiness, was their endless unpacking and rearranging. It seemed like they'd never put away all of the stuff.

Friday morning, Ginger's mother said, "Enough! Let's pack for Disneyland. We'll leave after Lilabet's nap."

"Disneyland!" Lilabet called out. "Disneyland!"

Even Joshua grinned, and Ginger yelled, "Disneyland, here we come!" She vowed not to give school another thought.

6

They arrived at their hotel near Disneyland in time to settle into their adjoining rooms before dinner. Grant and Joshua shared one room, and Mom got to sleep in what Grant called "the girls' room."

"Where's Disneyland?" Lilabet asked as she looked around the rooms, confused.

Everyone laughed, and Grant drew the draperies. "Look out the window."

In the distance, above the trees, were Matterhorn Mountain, Cinderella's Castle, the monorail, and whirling sky rides.

"Disneyland!" Lilabet crowed.

Ginger felt like yelling with excitement herself, and she could see that Katie did, too.

Grant promised, "We'll be there when they open tomorrow morning. Tonight we'll watch the fireworks from our rooms."

They walked to a nearby restaurant for dinner. Sitting beside Katie, Ginger tried to recall Disneyland from her visit four years ago. "We'll ride Space Mountain and Thunder Mountain and Star Tours and the Matterhorn ride. I can't wait!"

"I can't wait to see the castle!" Katie said.

"It's just a plain castle," Ginger told her. "There's no ride with it." She realized she didn't know Katie too well yet. "Don't you like rides?"

"I surely do," Katie answered, a little embarrassed. "It's . . . well, I've always seen the castle on TV."

"Tomorrow we'll see it for real," Ginger assured her. Last time she and Mandy Timmons had gone on all the best rides. She hoped Katie wasn't just a castle type.

Later, from their hotel room windows, they watched brilliant fireworks explode in the night sky above Disneyland. The bright bursts of color highlighted the castle's towers.

"Hey, just like on TV!" Katie exclaimed.

"Yeah," Ginger said, thrilled herself. If it were up to her, she'd be there right now, but Lilabet had to get a good night's sleep.

When they went to bed, she didn't think she'd ever fall asleep. It seemed like a strange slumber party with Mom, Lilabet, and Katie in the room, but it was fun and cozy, too. And it helped to have Katie along because Ginger didn't feel like the only outsider in the family. Best of all, she and Katie were getting to be better friends.

The next morning, they parked their car in the enormous Disneyland parking lot and caught a tram to the ticket booths at the front gate. Mom snapped pictures of all of them. "You all look so special," she told them.

Ginger thought she and Katie looked perfect in their white shorts, tank tops, and sandals. Katie looked best since she wasn't all knees, elbows, and freckles. Lilabet looked cute in her white shorts and a yellow T-shirt with a railroad crossing that said, STOPS AT ALL COOKIE JARS.

"Look!" Lilabet shouted, pointing to the monorail circling quietly overhead. "Disneyland!"

"It's like a dream," Ginger said as they waited in line by the front gate to buy their all-day passes.

Beside her, Lilabet piped, "I wanna see Mickey Mouse!"

"Hold on," Grant said, grinning as he handed out their passes. "Patience, Lilabet."

At last Ginger pushed in through the turnstile. "Here we are, Katie!" she exclaimed, her heart pounding.

Just above was the Main Street Station of the Disneyland Railroad, where the train stood huffing and puffing. Its bell rang, and the conductor yelled, "All aboooaaard!"

Katie sounded more southern than ever as she laughingly said, "Hey! Ah cain't believe Ah'm really heah!"

They all laughed, sharing her pleasure.

"Let's get a stroller," Mom said, "even if Lilabet doesn't want to ride now. There's the rental shop."

"No stroller!" Lilabet objected. "I'm a big girl."

Mom explained, "We'll just use it to carry the sweaters we brought for this evening. Come on!"

Excited, they hurried through the entry area and then through the railroad tunnel. As they stepped out into the sunlight, everything was like Ginger remembered, but she still thought *Wow!*

Quaint street lamps and colorful, old-fashioned buildings lined Town Square. Everywhere they looked, they saw gift shops, theaters, arcades, candy stores, and food stands. Disneyland music filled the air, and kids with Mickey Mouse-eared balloons and hats milled with their parents on the cobbled circle. Antique cars honked comically and a red fire engine clanged as they circled around with visitors.

"Mickey Mouse!" Lilabet squealed. "Mickey Mouse!" Jubilant, she pointed at the costumed mouse character. He was smiling, dressed just like in the cartoons: white shirt, yellow bow tie, black jacket, red pants.

Mickey waved, then ambled toward them in his enormous shoes. He reached out a big white-gloved hand to Lilabet who, to Ginger's amazement, suddenly turned bashful.

64

"Lilabet, how about shaking Mickey's hand?" Grant said.

Lilabet nodded shyly and reached out her hand. Katie shook his hand next, then Ginger had to herself.

Mom held up the camera. "Let's get a picture of you kids with Mickey."

Ginger and Katie giggled. "We're too old for that."

"No, you're not," Mom replied. "Joshua, you, too."

"Not me," he objected, retreating toward Grant.

Ginger asked Mickey, "Don't you talk?" and he shook his head from side to side.

"Mice don't talk," Joshua teased. "Even you know that, Ginger Trumbell."

"Just because you think you're so old!" She wrinkled her nose at him, then turned to smile as Mom snapped the picture. Why did Joshua have to call her Ginger *Trumbell*. Her last name set her apart from the Gabriels.

Mickey reached for Joshua's hand.

"Ha!" Ginger flung at Joshua as Mom snapped his picture.

Joshua scowled, and Ginger guessed it was because his friend couldn't come, and maybe other reasons. Maybe about her and Mom being with them.

After a while Mickey waved good-bye and ambled off toward other visitors. Still wide-eyed, Lilabet turned to solemnly inform them, "That was Mickey Mouse."

"You're kidding, Lilabet." Ginger laughed to cheer herself up. She remembered the Fourth of July when she'd gone on the fair rides with Joshua. He hadn't acted grumpy there, but she hadn't moved into his house yet then, either.

"We're off to a good start," Grant observed, as if he didn't notice the strain between Ginger and Joshua. "Let's plan our day."

"Let's go to Tomorrowland for Space Mountain first," Joshua suggested. "Last time I was here, we waited in line for an hour. Everybody says it's best to go in the morning."

Ginger shot him a don't-you-think-you're-smart look.

"Just what I had in mind," Grant replied. "First Tomorrowland, then Fantasyland, New Orleans Square, Adventureland, and Frontierland. How does that sound to everyone?"

They all agreed and started down Main Street.

Minutes later they were marveling at Tomorrowland, which gleamed with futuristic buildings and space-age rides. The monorail skimmed by overhead, and people screamed with delight from a rocket ride whizzing high in the air.

Mom and Lilabet set off to see a tame attraction, and the rest of them lined up for Space Mountain. The outer-space surroundings were so interesting that they didn't mind the line. Before long, they descended into a narrow corridor, which opened into a huge dark space station for rocket car departures. It was so realistic Ginger felt like they really were leaving on a ride through the universe.

"Ginger and Katie first," Grant said when their rocket car arrived. "Josh and I will sit in the seats behind you. We'll grab you if you start to float away up in space."

"Maybe we'll save *you*," Ginger shot back laughingly as they climbed into their seats.

Their rocket started off, climbing slowly through laser-lit tunnels, then they began to descend into darkness. Soon they were roller coastering and spiraling through stars and planets, whirling wildly through space. Somewhere ahead, other riders squealed, then Katie and Ginger found themselves shrieking wildly. Even Grant and Joshua were yelling behind them.

It was a long ride, and as their rocket braked to a stop on the track, Ginger caught her breath. "I wish we could go on it again!"

"Me, too," Katie agreed. "Wasn't that wild!"

When they stepped out into the sunlight, Mom and Lilabet stood waiting for them at the exit. "Was it fun?" Mom asked.

"Was it ever!" Grant exclaimed with the rest of them.

Lilabet interrupted their excitement with a proud, "Look what I got." She pointed with both hands at the hat on her head.

Katie exclaimed, "Hey, Lilabet, a Mickey Mouse hat!"

"Come on, Star Tours is next," Joshua said impatiently.

An hour later, when they rode the elevated People Mover overlooking Tomorrowland, Grant said, "I do believe we've gone on every ride below. Onward to Fantasyland, then we'd better think about lunch. Let's head for the castle."

Ahead of Ginger, she saw Grant pushing Lilabet in her stroller, and Mom walking companionably with Joshua. They were beginning to be more of a family today, even if Joshua was acting too important.

In Fantasyland, Katie pointed at another costumed character. "It's Cinderella! I can't believe this! I wonder if we can write reports on this for school?"

Ginger cringed. Why did Katie have to mention school when she was trying so hard to forget all about it? Determined not to think about it, she turned her attention back to their surroundings.

After strolling through the castle, Mom took Lilabet on the Dumbo Flying Elephants and the crazily whirling Tea Cups while Ginger and the rest of them rode Mr. Toad's Wild Ride, slam-banging in their miniature old-fashioned car through a rickety spook house.

As they continued through Fantasyland, Katie looked curious. "What's the big topsy-turvy place?"

68

She pointed at the whimsical building with clocks, wooden soldiers, spinning propellers, and swinging pendulums.

"Small World," Mom replied. "It's one of my favorites."

"It's kind of a girlish ride," Joshua said unpleasantly.

"That's not so, Josh," his father said. "I like it myself. Besides, we've all been humoring you quite a lot this morning. Let's remember to do unto others as you'd have them do unto you."

Joshua's face turned red. "Well, what about Ginger? You're always favoring her!"

"They do not!" Ginger shot at him.

"Kids!" Grant warned. "We're trying very hard not to favor anyone. If anyone feels badly treated, he or she can talk to me privately. We're here today to have a good time before school starts."

Why does everyone have to keep mentioning school? Ginger thought. It was only two days away now.

By the time they climbed into their Small World canal boat, Joshua had turned more pleasant. As they floated into the whimsical building, the cheerful music helped put Ginger in a happier mood. Dolls from around the world danced and sang, "It's a small world after all . . . it's a small world after all . . ."

At lunchtime, they sat outside eating hamburgers and admiring the colorful New Orleans Square

69

scene. Nearby, steam billowed from the smokestack of the big white Mark Twain Steamboat as it navigated around Tom Sawyer Island.

Grant said to Ginger, "It's your turn now. What would you like to see next?"

"Yo ho, yo ho, the pirates' life for me!" she sang out crazily. "Pirates of the Caribbean!"

He chuckled. "Then that's where we'll go."

By mid-afternoon, they'd visited all of New Orleans Square and most of Frontierland. They stopped for lemonade, then it was onward to Adventureland for the Tiki Room, Jungle Cruise, and Swiss Family Tree House.

It was already early evening when they rode Thunder Mountain. On the runaway mine train, they roared through a gold mining mountain, shaking through an earthquake and a thundering avalanche.

When the ride ended, they walked out and the aroma of Mexican cooking wafted through the air.

"Oh, that smells good," Grant said, "and just in time for dinner."

"Sounds wonderful!" Mom said. "I'm starved."

"Me, too!" Ginger said, almost drooling at the smells.

A colorful mariachi band played Spanish music at the outdoor restaurant with umbrella-covered tables. Spotting an empty table, Ginger dashed over to claim it.

Katie and Joshua sat down on either side of her,

and Mom and Grant across from them. Lilabet dozed by Mom in the stroller, her mouth hanging open.

When everyone was settled, Mom leaned over and kissed Grant's cheek. "Thanks for being a good guy," she said.

He grinned, pleased. "Thanks to you for being a good wife and mother."

E-m-b-a-r-r-a-s-s-i-n-g, Ginger thought. She shot a sideways glance at Katie, wondering if her parents, who were older, acted like that. Probably not, judging from Katie's odd smile.

Grant said to Mom, "Now, if I can convince you and Josh to help me carry out our orders, we'll leave Ginger and Katie to guard Lilabet and the table."

When they left, Ginger and Katie enjoyed the mariachi music and the sunshine slanting through the trees and table umbrellas. Katie talked about what a good day she'd had, but Ginger grew more and more tense. Their day at Disneyland was almost over, and she'd have to know soon about where to go to school.

Finally the others returned and passed around the chicken enchilada dinners. As Grant handed Ginger hers he asked, "Did you have a good day?"

"I sure did. Thanks."

"I'm glad," he said, his smile reaching all the way to his grayish-blue eyes. He turned serious. "Today's Saturday. I hate to mention it, Ginger, but school starts on Monday. Are you still praying about it?"

71

"I've prayed over and over," she told him. "I don't know why God doesn't answer."

"He will," Grant promised. "He will, and you'll know."

But He hadn't answered, and she didn't know! Probably she should honor Mom's and Grant's wishes, she thought. Maybe Santa Rosita Christian wouldn't be too bad, not with Katie and even Joshua around. Still, Dad didn't want her to go.

Grant said, "Let's say grace."

Bowing her head, Ginger joined hands with Katie and Joshua.

"Heavenly Father," Grant began, "we thank You for this day. It's our first real outing as a family. It's been a special outing, and we thank You for that . . . and for the love we already have for each other. We pray that You would help our love grow ever stronger. And, Father, we thank You for this food. In Christ's name we pray. Amen."

And, God, Ginger added silently, *please, tell me where I should go to school! I don't want to go to a new school, but I'll go wherever You want me to!*

She opened her eyes slowly. The sun shone through the trees and table umbrellas at a new angle, enfolding Mom and Grant with her in its golden ray. It seemed like a wondrous moment that God had created for just the three of them. Before it was over, Ginger knew without a doubt what God wanted her to do.

As though from far away, she heard her own

voice say to them, "I think God wants me to go to Santa Rosita Christian."

Strangely enough, once the words were out, she realized that God had changed her heart. Santa Rosita Christian was truly where she wanted to be.

7

Sunday after church, Ginger reread the letter she'd received on her return from Disneyland. Finally she'd heard from Mandy Timmons, her best friend until she'd moved to Chicago in June. Just seeing Mandy's handwriting made the day feel good.

After lunch, Ginger put on her bathing suit and took her stationery to the patio table. Sitting down, she took out a sheet of yellow paper. On top, a green parrot squawked: HERE'S THE LATEST FROM GINGER ANNE TRUMBELL! She began to write.

Dear Mandy,

I was so happy to get your letter. I'm glad you like living in Chicago. I was afraid you forgot me, but I guess you were

74

busy this summer, too. I wanted to answer right away because school starts tomorrow.

When I wrote to you in June, Mom and Grant Gabriel (the high school principal at Santa Rosita Christian) were only in love. Yup, they've gotten married! At first, I almost had a fit (Gram's words), then I got used to it. Would you believe I was the junior bridesmaid at the wedding? Surprise, surprise! It turned out to be nice!

I have a new address, too. We moved to Grant's house last week. Maybe I'll miss the beach, but we've been too busy so far. Yesterday we went to Disneyland. It reminded me of last time when I went with you. We had fun this time, too, and I got to take the new girl next door, Katie Cameron. She's a lot of fun, but not as crazy as you. Here's even bigger news. I'm a Christian! I can't believe it myself. Now that I see what it's like, I wish I'd given my heart to Jesus a long time ago. Here's another surprise. Tomorrow I start school at Santa Rosita Christian. I'm excited and a little scared. Grandfather Gabriel, a retired minister who lives out back in the guest house, says God will help me.

God has to help me, too, with my stepbrother, Joshua, who's in sixth grade. He *doesn't like me now that I've moved into the house. Lilabet, my stepsister, is three and a cute rascal. Between them and being a new kid at school, God has lots of helping to do.*

School is sure going to be different. Here's girls' dress rules from the handbook. "Knee-length dresses or skirts with neat blouses or sweaters. No T-shirts or tank tops. Enclosed toe and heel shoes. Socks required."

Can you imagine me wearing dresses and skirts to school? No weird clothes! The other rules look strict, too. Grant says it's good to be disciplined. Oh, Mandy, you know how I snap!

Here comes the family to swim in the pool. Oops, I forgot. I learned to swim, too.

Please write soon.

Your forever friend,
Ginger

The next morning, Ginger chewed her gum hard as she hurried to Grant's car. Katie had already climbed into the back.

"Hey, don't you look nice," she said.

"You think so?" Ginger asked as she swung her book bag into the backseat. She glanced at her white blouse, blue denim skirt, white socks and tennies. "I'm not used to wearing a skirt to school."

76

"What would you wear to your old school?"

Ginger shrugged. "Probably shorts, a T-shirt, and sandals. That's what kids wear there when it's hot like today."

"Don't they have air-conditioning?" Katie asked.

"Sure. That's just what we wore anyway." She eyed Katie's outfit. "You look nice yourself."

"Thanks," Katie said. She wore a yellow-and-white checkered blouse, yellow skirt, yellow socks, a yellow band around her ponytail, and white tennies. She looked perfect for what the school dress rules called "a God-honoring spirit." Ginger thought maybe tomorrow she'd wear a more colorful outfit herself.

Grant and Joshua rushed out to the car, Mom and Lilabet following behind them. Climbing into the car, Grant said, "Everyone excited about the first day of school?"

Ginger groaned comically with Katie.

Joshua ignored them, and Ginger thought he probably didn't like sharing his father's attention with them. Last year, just the two of them had ridden to school together.

Mom and Lilabet called, "Bye, Ginger! Bye, Katie! Have a good day."

"You, too, Mom!" Ginger yelled out her window.

Mom beamed. "Thanks!" Today she was starting art classes at Santa Rosita Community College. With Lilabet at home and such a big family now, Mom wasn't going to work for a while.

As they drove away, Grant said, "Don't forget, Josh, to ride home with Katie's mother after school. You won't have to spend the whole afternoon at school waiting for me this year."

Joshua nodded, but he didn't say a word all the way to school. Ginger suspected that trouble was brewing—not that she was going to worry about it. It was enough just to be going to a new school. She gave her gum a nervous crack.

"Here we are," Grant said as they arrived at the sprawling grounds of the old hillside school. "Josh, will you give me a hand with my things?"

Once they were under way, Ginger and Katie started up the walk to the white elementary building. Katie said, "Best of all, I like the big trees here. How about you?"

"Yeah." Ginger chewed her gum hard. "Yesterday after church Grant showed me our classroom."

"I saw it when we enrolled," Katie said. "The buildings surely are spread out."

"It seems strange to have a chapel at school." Ginger eyed the chapel, half-hidden by big California pepper trees. "Dad wouldn't like that at all."

At the white elementary building, a sign by Room 502 said, *Welcome to Fifth Grade!* A smiling young woman stood at the door. "Good morning, girls," she said in a soft, friendly voice. "I'm Miss Nordstrom. I'm the fifth-grade teacher, and I look forward to getting to know you."

"I'm Katie Cameron," Katie said, and Ginger

78

said, "I'm Ginger Trumbell."

Miss Nordstrom wore a pretty suit as bright blue as her eyes and a matching ribbon to hold back her light brown hair. Sometimes on the first day of school teachers seemed nervous, but this one was calm and looked eager to know them.

Ginger asked, "Are you a Christian?"

"Yes, I am," Miss Nordstrom answered, surprised.

"I thought so," Ginger said, though she couldn't figure out why. She gave her gum a pensive crack.

Miss Nordstrom smiled widely. "I enjoy chewing gum, too, Ginger. In fact, I like to blow bubbles, but it's against our rules here."

"Oh." Heat rushed to Ginger's face. "I guess you want me to throw it in the wastebasket."

"No, you can save it for after school if you like," Miss Nordstrom said. "It's a shame to waste perfectly good gum."

"It's old, so I guess I'll get rid of it," Ginger decided.

"If you like," Miss Nordstrom said.

A teacher who chews gum and blows bubbles! Ginger thought. She tossed her gum into the wastebasket.

Miss Nordstrom said, "I've seated you in alphabetical order, if you'd like to find your desks. Then you might like to go outside, since we start there with the pledge of allegiance."

Ginger told her, "I know how to say that."

Katie shot her an Are-you-crazy? glance. As they

started off to find their desks, she whispered, "Why do you say things like that?"

"Like what?"

Katie answered, "Like asking Miss Nordstrom if she's a Christian, and saying you know the pledge of allegiance!"

"I guess it was dumb," Ginger said.

Katie nodded. "It surely was."

"At least I don't say 'hey!' for everything and talk southern!" Ginger snapped.

Katie's brown eyes filled with hurt, and she blinked hard.

"I'm sorry," Ginger apologized. "Actually, I like to hear your southern accent."

"It's okay," Katie said, but Ginger knew that it wasn't.

Miss Nordstrom said, "Girls, since you're both new to Santa Rosita Christian, I'd like you to meet Dorene Castelle. I'm sure she'd be pleased to show you around school today."

Ginger turned and beheld the most beautiful girl she'd ever seen. Dorene Castelle was tall and slim and graceful as a princess. Her eyes were as blue-violet as pansies, and her wavy dark hair fell softly over her shoulders. She wasn't a girl who'd talk dumb.

Dorene said, "I'd be happy to show you around."

Katie had already found her desk in the front row, and Dorene said, "Good, you'll be sitting next to me. We're both C's."

Ginger found her own desk. As usual, it was in the back row with the other end-of-the-alphabet kids.

Dorene said, "There's the whistle for us to go out to the blacktop. We start school by the flags there."

Katie sounded more southern than ever. "We surely do appreciate your showing us around, Dorene."

Ginger followed them out, feeling all knees and elbows. A wonder she hadn't tripped over her own feet already.

Mr. Adams, the elementary principal, stood by the flagpole and waited for everyone to settle down. "Welcome back to Santa Rosita Christian, those of you who were students here last year," he said. "And a special welcome to our newcomers. I hope you old-timers will make our new students feel especially welcome. And now shall we pledge our allegiance?"

To Ginger's surprise, the second flag on the pole wasn't the California flag. Once they'd finished the pledge to the American flag, everyone said, "I pledge allegiance to the Christian flag and to the Savior for whose kingdom it stands. One Savior, crucified, risen, and coming again."

Well, she thought, *I don't know that one!*

Mr. Adams made the announcements, and everything sounded new and confusing. Finally, he dismissed them to their rooms.

In class, Ginger sat between two boys, Jonathan

Taylor and Daniel Wirt. They looked neat in their collared shirts and colored denim pants, and they acted friendly, even if they didn't want to sit by an all-knees-and-elbows girl.

Miss Nordstrom stood at the front of the room. "Good morning. Welcome to fifth grade. It's a pleasure to see those of you I met last year when you were in fourth grade, and I look forward to getting to know our newcomers. I've written our class schedule on the blackboard. We'll start the day with Bible—"

Start the day with Bible! Ginger's mind echoed.

Miss Nordstrom continued, "Our schedule includes social studies, science, math, reading, language, spelling, and handwriting." She smiled at them. "Why don't we begin with prayer? Who'd like to pray first?"

Ginger swallowed hard. Would she be expected to pray aloud? She bowed her head and folded her hands, listening to one of the girls pray as if it were the easiest thing on earth to do. When she finished, other kids prayed about school and for Miss Nordstrom and the class.

Miss Nordstrom finished with, "Heavenly Father, help us to acquire not only knowledge this year, but Your wisdom. Help us to remember how much You love us . . . and help us to love each other. In Jesus' name we pray. Amen."

Finally they passed out the textbooks. Sure enough, Ginger thought, here was a Bible to put in her desk with the other books. Even a Bible study workbook.

In between textbook passing and putting away, she glanced around. Lots of little things differed from her old school. A Christian flag hung on one side of the front wall, and behind her, on a bulletin board, a small sign said, "Wise men store up knowledge. Proverbs 10:14." Another said, "Study to show thyself approved by God. II Timothy 2:15." On the supply closet door, near Miss Nordstrom's desk, a sign said,

WISDOM

Isaiah 55:9

As the heavens are
higher than the earth, so
are my ways higher than
your ways and my thoughts
than your thoughts.

THINK GOD'S WAY

Little things or not, Ginger guessed they'd make a big difference. She'd have to learn her way around and get to know all of these kids. On top of that, she'd have to get to know the Bible and prayers and thinking God's way. How would she ever do all of it?

When school ended for the day, she felt wilted.

Katie's mother picked them up in her car out by the parking lot. She asked in her soft southern voice, "How was your first day of school?"

"Wonderful!" Katie exclaimed. "The kids are as friendly as they are in Georgia!"

Like Dorene Castelle, Ginger thought, jealous. Dorene liked Katie a lot, and Katie liked Dorene, too. Katie was always friendly and interested in others, but Ginger felt like yelling Lilabet's famous words, "You hurt my feelings!"

Mrs. Cameron asked, "Do you think you'll like it heah at school, Gingah?"

"I guess so," Ginger answered, not too sure.

Joshua, of course, liked school fine since he was a good student. He was already excited about the science fair.

When they arrived home, Mom said, "Freshly baked chocolate chip cookies! Lilabet and I thought we'd make a special treat for you when we came home. But I'm not going to spoil you, so don't expect them every day. Now tell me about school."

While eating the cookies and drinking apple juice, they told Mom about school. After they'd finished, Mom told about her art classes and said, "I think I'm going to love them."

After a while Joshua asked, "Where's Lilabet?"

"She was sleeping the last time I peeked in," Mom said. "Our cookie baking gave her a late start on her nap."

"Maybe I'll do my homework now," Ginger decided and finished her milk. She headed for her bedroom and opened the door.

"Oh!" Lilabet cried out.

If ever anyone looked guilty, it was Lilabet. She stood on the window seat, holding a small shell in one hand. The seashell collection was a jumble.

"What are you doing in my room?" Ginger demanded.

Lilabet screwed up her face, ready to yell.

"Never mind bawling!" Ginger warned. "The last thing I need now is to hear you bawling!"

Lilabet slowly handed the shell to her. "Here, Gin-ger." She looked scared, but grouchy and tired, too.

"I'll bet you haven't napped at all," Ginger guessed. "You'd better go to bed now if you don't want to get into trouble."

Lilabet nodded, then marched out through their connecting bathroom, Ginger right behind her.

"You're not supposed to come in my room unless I'm here and I say so," Ginger reminded her. "Do you understand that?"

Lilabet's shoulders hunched up, but she didn't answer.

"I guess it's my fault, too," Ginger admitted. "I probably forgot to lock my side of the door." She watched her little stepsister climb into bed. Lilabet pulled the bed sheet over her head and rolled over toward the wall.

"Sleep tight," Ginger said, pleased that she hadn't lost her temper entirely.

She returned to her room and locked her side of the connecting bathroom door. Looking around her bedroom carefully, she saw a small broken shell on the floor. No wonder Lilabet looked so guilty.

Ginger picked it up. It was only an ordinary seashell, and there'd be more like it at the beach. She'd get one for Lilabet, too, when she went to Gram's next Saturday. Maybe she'd start a shell collection for Lilabet.

She dumped her book bag on her bed and flopped down beside it on the white chenille bedspread. Lying there, she admired her stuffed animals on their bookshelf: Spider, Octopus, Dinosaur, Fish, Fair Lion, and Parrot, who still held the Bible verse card that began, "Put on the new self."

Had she really put on a new self? she wondered. Was she really a Christian? Sometimes she trusted the Lord with her life, but not always.

She guessed she still had an awful lot to learn.

8

Gingerly, gingerly—that's how to act the first few days at school, Ginger told herself. When she returned home from school, she was careful with Lilabet and Joshua, too. When she and Katie rode to and from school, she pretended Dorene hadn't come between them. Yet, gingerly as she acted, it was hard to be the new kid everywhere.

At school during lunchtime, everyone ate at the picnic tables on the blacktop. On Thursday, Dorene asked Ginger, "Haven't I seen you somewhere before?"

"I don't think so," Ginger answered. She bit into her red delicious apple. It was crisp and juicy.

"Maybe on the beach?" Dorene suggested. "I

spent most of the summer there. We live just a few blocks from it now."

"I used to live there, too," Ginger told her.

Dorene's blue-violet eyes widened with recognition. "I know! You're the girl who almost drowned!"

Ginger choked on her apple. "What?"

"She looked a lot like you . . . red curly hair and freckles all over," Dorene said.

Everyone looked at Ginger. Her words came out strangled. "It must have been someone else!"

"She sure did look like you," Dorene said.

"Well, it wasn't me!" Ginger snapped. "I'm a good swimmer!" That wasn't quite honest either, but it made her first lie sound more true.

"Come on," Katie put in, "let's practice kicking a soccer ball."

Relieved, Ginger said quickly, "PE's right after lunch anyhow." She crunched up her lunch bag and tossed it into the garbage can. A perfect shot. That'd help show them she wasn't the kind of kid who'd almost drown.

As they hurried down to the playing field, she began to worry about Katie. Grant had taught them both to swim this summer. Katie probably knew she'd lied.

Down on the playing field, Ginger kicked the ball hard. It flew across the grass way down the field. She heard a boy say, "Ginger might be the best girl player here this year."

Maybe I am! she wanted to yell, but she didn't. She'd lied minutes ago, but at least now she'd practiced a little of what Grant called self-control.

Friday, riding home with Katie's mother, Katie said, "Dorene invited me to go to the beach with her tomorrow."

Ginger's heart sank, but she said, "I'll be there, too. I'll be visiting my *father* and *grandmother*." She didn't know why she'd called Dad and Gram that except it sounded good. Since Dorene was so special, it seemed important to impress Katie—even if Dad didn't show up.

"I might see you there," Katie said.

"Maybe," Ginger replied, unsure whether she hoped so or not. At least Dorene didn't go to their church, so she wouldn't be with Katie in Sunday school.

On Saturday morning, Grandfather Gabriel drove Ginger to Gram's house in his white Plymouth. "Something seems to be troubling you, Ginger," he remarked as they pulled off the beach freeway exit. "I hope it isn't your new school."

"I like school and Miss Nordstrom," Ginger answered, "but—" she hesitated. Grandfather had kept her secrets, like when she'd accepted the Lord, and she really did need to tell someone. "It's . . . well, it's about Katie. Another girl is stealing her away from me, and it's getting worse and worse!"

"I'm sorry to hear that," he said. He kept his eyes

on the road. "Is she purposely trying to steal Katie away?"

Ginger stared out the window, too. "I guess not. It's just that Dorene's so perfect." Ginger remembered her own lie. "She's nicer and lots easier to like than I am."

"I'm sure she's not perfect, Ginger. Only the Lord is. But I know what you mean." Grandfather darted a sympathetic glance at her. "Some people seem to have especially gracious natures. You have a lot to offer as a friend, too."

"But Dorene always says the right thing," Ginger objected, "and I never think before I talk. She doesn't lose her temper like I do either."

"Hmmm," Grandfather said, "sounds like it's two problems. The first one is about friendship and the second is about temper. You know, Ginger, I'm proud of you. Not everyone will admit their problems. It shows you're growing."

"You think so?"

"I know so," he replied. "It's when you have problems that you can really grow as a person. Now, let's think of how best to handle those problems."

He was quiet for a long time, then he said, "You know, Jesus was always out looking for new friends, and we are to be like Him. Maybe there's another girl at school who's just waiting to be your friend, but neither of you know it yet."

"But I want to stay best friends with Katie!"

Grandfather said, "You can have more than one friend. I don't know what I'd do if I only had one special friend."

Ginger remembered having just Mandy Timmons for a good friend, then when she'd moved away there'd been no one else. "You really think I should have more than one special friend?"

"Of course." Grandfather raised his thick gray brows. "I wouldn't be surprised if there's someone in your class right now who'd like you for a special friend."

"But how will I find her?" Ginger asked.

"Sounds as though you'll have to be friendly to everyone to find out who it is, doesn't it?"

Ginger drew a deep breath. "Sometimes I don't know how to be friendly. Worst of all, I don't even like everyone."

"That's not so unusual. But I know a way to get around it," he said. "If you spend a lot of time talking to Jesus, it shows. He'll help you to love your neighbor as yourself."

"What about my bad temper?"

He gave a laugh. "There's never been a temper so bad that the Lord couldn't tame it. When you feel like yelling at someone, give your temper to Jesus. Say, 'Lord, I don't want this bad temper anymore.' And if you feel it rising up again, say it to Him again. For any kind of trouble, you can just say, 'Lord, I need Your help.' "

Ginger gave her gum a crack. "I'll try it."

She gazed out the window, thinking about Katie. Was she friendly to Dorene for a special reason? Maybe because Katie was what Mom called compassionate?

"Tell me some good things about school," Grandfather said.

"Well . . . Grant taught me the Christian pledge, so I know that now. And Bible class is a lot more interesting than I expected. PE is my favorite class, though, just like at Santa Rosita Elementary. I like English, too."

"It sounds as though some things are going well," he said.

As they drove up in front of Gram's house, he observed, "It looks as though your father is here."

Uh-oh, she thought, her heart sinking at the sight of his red sports car. He'd never been around on Saturdays all summer when she'd needed him, and now that she was going to Santa Rosita Christian, he'd be mad at her.

"We'll pick up you and Gram tomorrow for church," Grandfather said as she climbed out of the car. "Have fun."

"Thanks," she replied, slamming the car door.

Maybe things would be like they used to, she hoped. And if Dad left as usual after mowing the lawn, she wouldn't have to act so . . . gingerly.

Gram opened the door for her, looking perky and excited. Her salt-and-pepper curls gleamed, and Ginger guessed she'd washed her hair this morning.

"There you are, Ginger," she said. "I'm so glad to see you. How's your new school?"

"Fine, I guess."

"Wait till you see what I've got for you." Smiling, Gram headed for her living room couch. As usual, it was stacked high with fabrics and half-sewn clothing. "Your mom said you have to wear dresses and skirts at school, so I used your favorite color and coordinating prints."

"Wow, look at all of that!" Ginger exclaimed. Spread out on the back of the couch in her size was a dark green skirt, a matching blouse, a white blouse with peach and green swirls, and a top with comical green cats printed all over it.

"Next week I'll make you a peach skirt and blouse," Gram told her, "then you can really mix and match—" She stopped nervously as Dad stepped into the room.

"Hi, kiddo," he said to Ginger, not smiling at all. Instead, he pressed his lips together, which pulled down his thick dark moustache. His hair was damp and kinked up from mowing the lawn.

"Hi," she answered. "What—what's wrong?"

"What do you think?" he asked, his brown eyes flashing.

Gram broke in. "Never mind, Steve. Forget it."

Trying to avoid trouble between them, Ginger said, "Look at all the clothes Gram made me for school. I have to wear skirts instead of jeans now." He glared at her and, bewildered, she rushed on.

93

"Sometimes I can't even think what to wear, but these are all coordinated, so that'll help a lot. . . ."

His voice rasped, "You should have stayed at your old school, like I told you, and you wouldn't have to worry about this stuff."

"I—I'm sorry, Dad."

"Steve," he reminded her. "My name is Steve."

"I—I wasn't thinking."

"Well, don't forget it." His angry eyes held hers. Finally, he let out a deep breath as if he wanted to lighten up. "Well," he said, "no green fingernails?"

She smiled a little and glanced at her nails. "I guess I don't need 'em anymore."

"And what's that supposed to mean?" he asked.

"I'm getting too . . . old for that now."

He said, "I thought you were going to give me some stuff about your being a Christian."

Ginger shook her head. "No."

"Stop it, Steve," Gram warned. "Ginger's a lot happier since she's a Christian. It wouldn't hurt you to try it yourself. Your own life's such a mess that you wound people left and right without even—"

"Don't tell me you're one now, too!" he interrupted.

Gram lifted her chin. "I went to church last Sunday, and I intend to go tomorrow. Just because you're mad at God doesn't mean I have to be, too."

"What makes you think I'm mad at God?" he asked.

"Because you find fault with people who love

Him," Gram answered. "Why else would you always be looking for flaws? And why else would you object to Ginger being in a Christian school?"

"How do you know so much about it?" he demanded.

"I went to church when I was young, and I was happy as could be," Gram replied. "I should never have stopped going, but I got married and your father didn't want me to go."

"I suppose that's my fault!" he flared.

"No, it's not," Gram said, "but you're a lot like your father. You've even got his bad temper."

"Do I!" he retorted. "If I'm so awful, you better find someone else to mow the lawn and do all of the other dirty work, because I'm leaving."

Ginger snapped at him, "You're just trying to get out of helping! You want to fade away like you did last summer when I needed you. You always take off when there's trouble."

"Your mother has poisoned both of you against me!" he said angrily. "What has she told you about our divorce, anyway?"

"Nothing," Gram replied. "She's never told us a thing."

He said, "I'm asking Ginger."

"She's never explained, and she's never said a bad thing about you," Ginger told him, her heart aching. "Never ever."

"You do your own self in, Steve," Gram said.

He shot both of them a furious look, grabbed his

car keys off the table, and slammed out of the house, the screen door banging noisily behind him. Moments later, his car roared away.

"I'm sorry, Gram," Ginger finally said into the silence. "I lost my temper, too."

Gram shook her head, then sank down on the couch in the midst of her fabrics and sewing projects. "I lost my temper myself. Grown-ups can make an awful mess of things, too."

"It wouldn't have happened if I hadn't come," Ginger said.

"No," Gram replied. "Your father was mad when he walked in that door. He has his own troubles, but part of it, I expect, is because you and your mother have good, new lives. I think he's plain resentful."

Ginger sat down beside Gram on the couch and took her hand. "I love you, Gram," Ginger said. "I love you a lot."

Gram gave her a hug. "Oh, Ginger, I love you, too. I don't know what I'd do without you."

They gazed at each other ruefully.

The hot autumn wind gusted in through the screen door, banging it against the doorjamb. "I'd better write Dad an apology," Ginger decided.

"I guess I should apologize, too," Gram said, "even though it wasn't my fault . . . or yours."

Ginger drew a discouraged breath. "Grandfather Gabriel just told me how to give my temper to the Lord, but I didn't even do it when I needed it."

"A lot of us forget when life gets difficult."

"Yeah," Ginger answered, "but I forget a lot."

Hard as she'd tried this week to live her life more gingerly, she'd not only lied to Dorene, but lost her temper. *Lord*, she prayed, *forgive me. And please, please help!*

9

Ginger was still asleep when she felt something warm and wet moving over her arm. A familiar smell filled her nostrils. She didn't want to wake up . . . Monday morning . . . school. She popped one eye open. Raffles. It was his warm, rough tongue. "You old rascal," she said.

He stared at her through long, shaggy hair, and his mouth turned up in a smile.

She sat up and asked, "Aren't you going to scratch yourself, you old fleabag?"

He did.

She rubbed his head, not quite sure when she'd begun to like him so much.

Mom poked her head in the door. "It looks like

98

Raffles wants to be your friend. I said, 'Raffles, go wake up Ginger,' and he started right down the hall for you."

At least that made *one* friend, Ginger thought.

"I was sorry to hear about the trouble with your father," Mom said. "Gram called me last night. When we drove to church, you were so quiet that she was concerned."

Ginger shrugged. At least she'd written him an apology yesterday after church.

"I wish I could change our past for you, Ginger," her mother said, "but I can't. We have to go on."

Ginger nodded.

"Which brings me to your birthday," Mom said. "It's only three weeks away. I thought you might like to have a special outing. Grant suggested the San Diego Wild Animal Park. We have some free tickets."

"Yeah," Ginger said, feeling better. "We haven't been there in ages."

"We could take some of your new friends from school and make a special occasion of it," Mom offered.

Ginger's spirits drooped. "I don't have many friends yet."

"But you will soon. There's Katie, and you said there are only ten girls in your class. It'd be a wonderful way to make friends with the eight other girls."

"You mean invite all of them?"

"Why not?" her mother asked.

Ginger felt tempted to tell about Katie liking Dorene best, about seeing them Saturday afternoon at the beach. She and Gram had walked there after lunch and, as if she hadn't felt terrible enough about Dad, she'd had to see Katie and Dorene being "best friends." She'd made plenty sure they didn't see her. So much for her "best friend."

Her mother said, "A good way to make friends is to ask about their interests. It takes an effort to make friends."

"I guess so," Ginger said.

Her mother added, "You have to be willing to be open with people, too. You know . . . tender and vulnerable. That means taking risks, taking chances on being rejected. And, of course, you can't force friendships. By the way, that was really thoughtful of you to start a shell collection for Lilabet. I've never seen anyone so excited about shells. I hope you don't mind her too much, Ginger."

"She's okay," Ginger said.

Later, while she dressed, she decided that Mom might be right. Having a birthday party would be a good way to make friends. She remembered Grandfather telling about Jesus always looking for new friends. Grandfather had said, "Maybe there's another girl at school who's just waiting to be your friend, but neither of you know it yet."

The next day at school Ginger listed all of the girls

in her class. The list, in alphabetical order by first name, read: *Anne-Marie Walters, Brenda Dupree, Cassie Davis, Dorene Castelle, Erika Gillespie, Julie Lenzkes, Katie Cameron, Lora Huckstep, and Marcia Schiwitz.*

She checked off Katie and Dorene, since she already knew them. That left seven. She'd start at the top of the list at recess with Anne-Marie Walters, who was blonde and always wore pink. She'd be easy because she was little and sweet. *Lord, help me to be friends with Anne-Marie Walters,* Ginger prayed.

At recess, Ginger headed for Anne-Marie instead of the playing field. Standing in front of her, she asked right out: "What's your biggest interest?"

Anne-Marie blinked her blue eyes. "I guess I like art best, artistic things. Are you doing a—what do you call it—a survey?"

"Sort of." Ginger searched her brain for more to say, then had it. "You know, my mom likes to stencil ceiling borders and stuff. In fact, pretty soon she's going to paint the kitchen so she can stencil hearts and flowers all over like we had in our house by the beach."

"Really?" Anne-Marie asked. "I've thought about stenciling ceiling borders on some of the rooms in my dollhouse, but it'd be awfully hard to do."

"Your dollhouse?!" Ginger repeated. That sounded like something for little kids.

"It's big, not a babyish dollhouse," Anne-Marie

explained. "My grandfather made it, and it has miniature furniture and real lights and electricity. It's really neat."

By the time recess was over, Ginger had learned a lot about miniature furniture and other dollhouse stuff.

At noon, she ate lunch with Anne-Marie, who said, "Maybe you could come over sometime to see my dollhouse."

"Sure," Ginger answered, not knowing what else to say.

On Tuesday, Anne-Marie brought her a Polaroid picture of her dollhouse and, after admiring it, Ginger said, "Let's go show it to Brenda."

"To Brenda? You think she'd be interested?" Anne-Marie asked. "She's a . . . you know, a brain."

"Sure, she'd be interested," Ginger said, sounding more hopeful than she felt. Anyhow, Brenda was next on the making-friends list. Ginger eyed the kids out at recess and saw Brenda just coming out of their room.

"Brenda!" Ginger yelled.

Brenda turned, her brown eyes wide. She tossed her dark braid behind her shoulders. "Hi," she said.

"Hi," Ginger answered. "Hey, what's your big interest?"

Brenda blinked with surprise, too. "Writing, I guess."

"You mean you want to be a writer?"

"Maybe," Brenda said. She blushed a little, then added, "My grandma collects comic strips and cartoons about writing for me and sends them. It sounds kind of dumb."

"No," Ginger said. "Anne-Marie collects dollhouse miniatures, did you know that?"

"No, I didn't," Brenda said. "What do you collect, Ginger?"

"Mostly shells, but my grandma in Virginia sends me collectors' dolls from around the world . . . not for playing."

They grew so interested that the next thing Ginger knew, the recess bell was ringing.

Back at her desk, Ginger checked off Brenda's name. How about that! Brenda the Brain collected cartoons about writing!

Wednesday was easy since Cassie Davis liked sports, too. Ginger got Anne-Marie and Brenda playing kick ball with Cassie, who wanted to play soccer in the Olympics someday.

"Wow!" Ginger said, "I'd like to be in the Olympics, too!"

Thursday Ginger brought in Erika, who loved horses and wanted to be a vet. She told her about Raffles, the only animal she'd ever known. "He's been waking me up every morning this week," Ginger said. "He's an old fleabag, but I like him anyway." Telling that had been "open" and "vulnerable."

Julie and Lora were best friends. Julie took ballet

lessons, and Lora liked to sing. Ginger spent Friday recesses and lunch hour with them. "I'm making a survey," she explained.

"Oh?" Julie asked, darting a glance at Lora.

They probably thought she was crazy, Ginger decided. Anyhow, she'd already known they were best friends, but no one could say she hadn't tried. Mom said you couldn't force friendship.

Marcia Schiwitz was number seven. Her grandma had died last year, so it wasn't surprising she wanted to be a nurse. Ginger reported to Anne-Marie, "Marcia wants to be a nurse."

Anne-Marie said to Marcia, "You'll look good in a white uniform with your black hair and blue eyes."

Ginger explained to Marcia, "Anne-Marie is artistic."

Two weeks after listing the girls in her class, Ginger decided her making-friends idea wasn't perfect. While she went on making new friends, the others paired off, even if they stayed friendly to her. But the real trouble was, she still wanted Katie to be her best friend.

Friday after school, Ginger and Mom bought birthday party invitations with a green parrot on the front. He squawked, "HERE'S AN INVITATION TO . . ." Inside, Ginger filled in all the party details. On Monday morning, she gave the first one to Katie on the way to school.

Katie beamed as she read it. "What a good idea—going to the Wild Animal Park for a birthday party. I surely do hope I can go." She hesitated, then added, "I hope you'll invite Dorene, too. She really needs friends—" She stopped as if she'd said too much.

Hurt, Ginger snapped, "I'm inviting every girl in our class. Every single one."

Katie looked hurt for a moment, too, then she smiled. "I didn't know it'd be such a big party. It surely does sound wonderful, like when y'all took me to Disneyland."

"Yeah," Ginger said, "yeah."

At school, she handed out the other invitations.

As she gave one to Dorene, Ginger blurted, "I lied to you. I was the girl who almost drowned. I was too embarrassed to tell the truth."

Dorene's blue-violet eyes almost popped.

"Anyway," Ginger said quickly, "I hope you'll come to my party this Saturday." She hurried away before Dorene could answer.

It didn't feel good to have confessed. And it sure was what Mom called taking a risk. On top of that, maybe everyone would guess about her making-friends list, Ginger worried. Maybe they'd know she'd done the "survey" so she'd have friends to invite to the party. What if they all figured it out and wouldn't come?

10

On Monday afternoon, Ginger overheard Anne-Marie asking Brenda, "What are you going to get Ginger for her birthday?"

"I thought she might like a really nice journal," Brenda confided. "When you get to be eleven, there's lots of important things to write down."

Anne-Marie asked, "Do you think she'd like miniatures like mine? She seemed interested in them."

"Probably," Brenda answered. "She's interested in all kinds of things."

They like me! Ginger thought. They even cared enough to want to give her special presents.

At home the next evening, she overheard Mom

talking to Gram on the phone. "I thought I'd make a chocolate cake with chocolate cream filling and frosting. You know Ginger and chocolate. I'll decorate it with yellow flowers and green leaves, and use yellow and green candles. What do you think?"

Sounds d-e-l-i-c-i-o-u-s, Ginger thought. This would be the best birthday of her life. And she'd finally be eleven years old. She hoped Dad would remember, too; she hadn't seen him since their fight three weeks ago.

At school the girls buzzed with excitement all week about the party. "What should we wear?" Julie and Lora asked.

"No dresses or skirts like at school!" Ginger answered, and they all laughed like old friends.

Cassie said, "I'll bring along my soccer ball in case there's time to play when we're at your house."

Ginger didn't know when there'd be time for soccer before the Wild Animal Park, but she kept her mouth shut.

Every day the girls grew more excited.

On the way to school Friday morning, Katie said, "I can't wait till tomorrow for your party!"

"Me neither!" Ginger admitted, giving her gum a loud crack. The only trouble was that she didn't feel too well this morning. Even her fresh stick of gum tasted awful.

Katie asked, "Did you put makeup or some other stuff on your face?"

"No," Ginger answered. "What do you mean?"

Katie said, "Your cheeks look red."

Ginger felt her cheeks. They were really hot. "Maybe I scrubbed too hard this morning."

She saw Grant eye her in the rearview mirror. "Do you feel all right, Ginger?" he asked.

"Sure," she answered, but inside she wasn't quite so positive. Her stomach felt queasy, and she was beginning to ache all over. She remembered that Jonathan Taylor, who sat beside her in class, had gotten sick at recess yesterday, and he'd had to go home early.

Even Joshua glanced at her from the front seat. "Your face is red all right. It's scarier than usual."

"Never mind!" she retorted.

"Josh, that's no way to talk," Grant said. "How about an apology?"

When they parked at school, Ginger felt so weak she barely made it to the elementary building. Usually she was out playing on the blacktop until the announcements, but this morning she wished she could sit inside at her desk.

Finally the bell rang, and somehow Ginger made it through the pledges of allegiance. Her knees felt wobbly during the announcements, but she made herself stand.

At last, she could go to the classroom.

"Good morning to you," Miss Nordstrom said from the front of the room. She wore her pretty blue suit, the one she'd worn the first day of school. "I'd like you to work on your word warm-up first."

She returned to her desk and began to take the milk list. After a while she asked, "Ginger, would you like milk?"

The thought of drinking milk made Ginger feel sicker yet, but she managed a quiet "Yes, please." *I'll feel better soon*, she told herself. *I'll feel better soon.*

When the round clock above the blackboard said eight-thirty, Miss Nordstrom went forward to take prayer requests. Ginger felt so awful, she wished they'd pray for her.

Next, it was time for math class. "Ginger, John, and Martin, would you do the problems on the board?"

Ginger stood up slowly and started up the aisle. In front of her, Miss Nordstrom's face was spinning and so were the math problems on the blackboard.

Miss Nordstrom stepped forward. "Are you feeling well?"

Ginger's stomach rose up on her fast. Before she could even turn away, she threw up . . . all over Miss Nordstrom's beautiful blue suit skirt and the floor.

The class gasped, and Mrs. Nordstrom exclaimed, "Oh, Ginger!" She put her arm around her and said, "Let me help get you out into the fresh air."

As they started down the aisle, Miss Nordstrom added, "Brenda, please take charge of the room. You can all work on the math problems quietly.

And, Martin, would you please get the custodian and ask the office to call Mr. Gabriel, the high school principal?"

Somehow Ginger stumbled onward, being sick again in the wastebasket by the door. Finally they were outside. The fresh air made her feel better, but it didn't stop her awful embarrassment. She wished she could die, really and truly die.

"Feeling better?" Miss Nordstrom asked, concerned.

Ginger nodded. "I'm sorry, Miss Nordstrom. I'm so sorry."

"I know you are, Ginger. Don't worry, it'll be all right. Let me help you over to a table on the blacktop."

When they arrived at the table, Ginger laid her head down on her arms. Even though the sun was shining, she shivered.

Miss Nordstrom said, "I'll put my jacket over your back."

"I'm so sorry," Ginger apologized again.

"It's not your fault, Ginger. These things happen to everyone at one time or another."

Yeah, Ginger thought. At her old school, Victoria Bates had thrown up at recess, and everyone had called her Victoria Vomit all year. Now everything would be ruined at this school; she'd never have any friends.

It seemed forever until Grant arrived. He sounded breathless. "How are you feeling, Ginger?"

"Not good," she muttered without looking up.

Miss Nordstrom said, "There's a three-day flu passing like wildfire through the elementary school."

"We have it over at the high school, too," Grant answered. "I'd better take Ginger home."

The school secretary arrived with wet paper towels, and Ginger shivered harder than ever as she tried to clean up. She tried not to see Miss Nordstrom's skirt.

Finally she climbed into Grant's car, carrying extra paper towels just in case. It was a good thing, too, because Grant had to stop for her to be sick alongside the freeway. Now everyone in Santa Rosita would know and be disgusted.

When Grant helped her into the house, Mom was in the kitchen with Lilabet, and they were whipping up a chocolate cake. Ginger's stomach churned wildly at the smell. Suddenly she remembered: *Tomorrow is my birthday! Tomorrow! This is my birthday cake!*

The house seemed to whirl around her, then she was in her bathroom and Mom was helping her wash up. At long last Ginger was in her pajamas and shivering under her blankets. She hadn't opened her drapes that morning, so the room was still dark. If only she'd never gotten out of bed!

"I'll call the doctor," Mom said. "Try to sleep."

When Ginger awakened hours later, it was already late afternoon. "Are you awake, Ginger?" her

111

mother asked softly from the doorway.

"I guess so. I've been dreaming bad, bad stuff, but I can't remember what it was."

"You'll be better soon," Mom promised. "I've brought you ginger ale. That's all the doctor wants you to have now."

"Okay," Ginger said, "but no ginger jokes."

"I promise," her mother said, then went over to open the draperies over the window seat. "The doctor wants you to rest for a few days."

"No birthday party?" Ginger asked.

"I'm afraid not, at least not now. Maybe in a few weeks."

Ginger moaned, "I don't want one at all."

"Now, Ginger—" Mom stopped and stared at the floor. "Oh, dear!"

Ginger rose up in bed and saw it: the special conch shell Mom and Grant had brought from their honeymoon, lying broken to pieces on the floor.

"Lilabet did it!" Ginger yelled. "She's always been after it!"

They glanced toward the hallway and saw Lilabet backing away guiltily.

Mom asked, "Have you been in Ginger's room, Lilabet?"

Lilabet screwed up her face and began to bawl.

Ginger pulled the covers over her head. "How could she? How could she?" After all of her trouble starting a shell collection for Lilabet, how could she come in and break the conch shell? How could so many bad things happen in one morning? What would go wrong next?

"I'll deal with Lilabet," Mom said, "and I'm sure Grant will, too. The best thing for you, Ginger, is sleep."

As awful as she felt, Ginger didn't see how she'd ever sleep. It was a long time before she dozed off.

The next morning, Grandfather Gabriel knocked at her door. "I've brought you some apple juice. It seems I'm the only one in the family who's still well."

Ginger made herself sit up in bed. "You mean everyone else is sick?"

"Every last one of them," he said. "Your Gram's coming over to help. The doctor says older people aren't getting this flu bug. He thinks we're immune to it."

"I sure hope so," Ginger said and sank back against her pillow. She'd not only disgraced herself everywhere, she'd made everyone in her whole family sick.

Grandfather smiled kindly. "I'm not sure I should say it, Virginia, but 'Happy Birthday.' "

"Thanks." She wanted to bawl like Lilabet. Ginger Anne Trumbell was eleven years old today, and it was the worst birthday of her life. If she couldn't die, she at least wanted to sleep. It was bad enough being sick, but a billion times worse to be so unhappy. Finally, she prayed, *Lord, help me. I don't want to feel so awful in my heart, too.*

113

That evening, when Ginger awakened, Gram was in the bedroom. "How are you feeling, Ginger?"

"A little better," she said.

Grandfather Gabriel joined them. "We have some surprises for you."

A few minutes later, it *was* surprising to see Mom and Grant and Joshua and Lilabet come into the room in their robes and pajamas. "Happy birthday to you. . ." they sang, but not too energetically. They looked so weak and wobbly that Ginger had to smile, especially when they sang the second verse. "No-more-birthdays-like-this to you, no-more-birthdays-like-this to you. . . ."

Grandfather said, "Now if this motley crew will be seated on the floor, I'll play master of ceremonies. We have lots of presents for the birthday girl. You all wait here."

After a moment, he and Gram carried in armloads of presents and stacked them on the foot of Ginger's bed. "They've been arriving all day, thanks to Katie," he said. "Now, first, here's a card from your teacher."

Ginger opened the card with trepidation, remembering Miss Nordstrom's ruined skirt.

Miss Nordstrom had drawn the card herself. The front pictured a redheaded girl with wild curls and only a few freckles. "Happy Birthday to One of My Favorite Students!"

Inside, Miss Nordstrom had written, "All of us

have prayed for you, and we know you'll be well soon. We took a vote, too. Everyone promises never to mention your getting sick in class to anyone ever, not even to you. Do you know why? Because we love you. You certainly have some good friends here already, Ginger. Get well soon."

Ginger blinked hard and set the card up on her nightstand.

Grandfather said, "First, I'll give you the presents from the girls who were coming to your party. They decided you should have them today instead of waiting until your delayed outing. This top one's from Katie."

On the envelope it said, "To my best friend, Ginger."

Ginger reread the words. "To my *best friend*, Ginger." *Best friend.*

She blinked hard again.

Inside, the card said, "I'm praying for you to get well soon. Your friend, Katie."

Ginger had to grab a paper tissue from her nightstand to blow her nose, then she opened the present. It was a beautiful book with colorful pictures of Disneyland.

Her grandmother asked, "Do you want me to pass it around?"

Ginger nodded and reached for another gift.

Anne-Marie's was a miniature couch with two tiny dolls on it, and Brenda's was a really good journal. Cassie gave her a soccer ball, and her note said,

"Get well soon so we can practice together!" Erika's gift was a small molded horse that would look just right on the bookshelf. Julie and Marcia both gave books; Julie's, about a girl who wanted to be a ballerina, and Marcia's, about a girl who wanted to be a nurse. Lora gave her a Gospel record. They all wanted to share what they liked best, Ginger thought. They really were friends!

"This envelope was with them," Gram said.

Ginger opened the envelope and found a pack of gum and a note. Dorene Castelle had written, "It was brave of you to say you lied about almost drowning in the ocean. I'm going to be honest, too. My father lost his job, and we've got lots of troubles, so I can't buy you a present now. I dreamed up excuses, then I knew I should tell the truth, too. Katie said you'd be my friend anyhow. Happy Birthday, Ginger! Get well soon! Your friend, I hope, Dorene Castelle."

So that's why Katie spent so much time with her, Ginger thought. It was just like Mom said, Katie was compassionate.

"Open our presents now, Ginger," Joshua urged. "Here, open mine." He handed it to her.

He'd made a card, too. He'd drawn a picture of a stick girl with wild red curls. "Happy Birthday to My New Sister, Ginger!" it said on the front. Inside, he'd drawn a ping-pong table and a stick-figure player with huge green fingernails. Below that, it said, "You're all right, Ginger, even if you are the world's best ping-pong player!" Inside the box was a pack of ping-pong balls.

"Thanks," she told him, and he nodded like he really did think she was bearable, stepsister or not.

Gram had made her a bright green dress with GINGER stitched on it, and Dad gave her a matching sweater. His card said, "I'll see you *for sure* next Saturday, kiddo. Get ready for a knuckle rub."

She swallowed hard. He'd forgiven her, just as she'd forgiven him. *Thank You, Lord,* she prayed.

Grandfather had two presents for her, and the first Ginger opened was a book about angels.

"How did you guess I wanted to know more about angels?" she asked him.

"I just knew. I hope you'll like my other gift, even though it's quite old."

It was the largest gift of all. Excited, Ginger tore off the wrappings and opened the cardboard box.

"An angel!" It was carved of wood, stained dark brown, and cracked here and there. It'd been carved by someone who believed in angels a long time ago, she decided. And since then, it'd been kept waxed by someone who probably believed in them, too.

"It belonged to my wife," Grandfather explained. "I know she'd be happy for you to have it."

"I'll take good care of it forever," Ginger said.

"I knew you would," he replied.

She thought it must be the most special present she'd received in her entire life.

Grandfather said, "I'd probably better put it up on your bookshelves so nobody breaks it."

"Thanks," Ginger said, darting a glance at Lilabet.

Mom and Grant gave her new peach pajamas and, just what she'd asked for—a pair of cowboy boots.

Mom said, "And we're giving the outing to the Wild Animal Park when we're all well."

Lilabet urged impatiently, "Open my present, Gin-ger."

Gram handed a big box to her and said, "This is from Lilabet, and she's made you a special card, too."

Lilabet had crayoned scrawls all over a ragged piece of paper, and Ginger remarked, "Isn't this nice writing!"

Lilabet explained, "It says, 'Gin-ger, I'm sorry' and 'Gin-ger, I love-love-love-love you.'"

"Thanks, Lilabet," Ginger said as forgiveness filled her heart. She unwrapped the box and pushed aside the tissue paper. "A conch shell—"

Grandfather said, "Lilabet wanted to buy it with her own money. I tried to find one just like the first."

"It does look like . . . the other," Ginger said. "This one may be even better."

"Blow it, Gin-ger!" Lilabet urged.

"Now?" Ginger asked.

Lilabet nodded hard. "Blow it now!"

118

Gathering up her strength and all her breath, Ginger raised the conch to her lips. She blew a mighty blast, and then another. *Aooooouuuuuh . . . aooooouuuuuh!* it sounded.

They all held their ears and laughed.

Her window stood open, and Ginger guessed the sound was floating through the neighborhood. *Aooooouuuuuh . . . aooooouuuuuh!*

Grant remarked, "You know, this one might be an improvement. It doesn't sound like a call to battle."

Ginger had to agree. It was more a call to peace . . . what she'd hoped for between her and all of them.

The next moment she recalled her prayer. *Help me . . . I don't want to feel so awful in my heart.*

God had truly changed things. He'd changed them through her friends and through her family.

She beamed at them, and joy rose in her heart.

They sure were a motley crew in their robes and pajamas, and today wasn't fun like going somewhere special or having a party would be. But it was a good birthday. She loved them and, more surprising, they loved her. She knew, because on all of their faces—Mom's, Grant's, Grandfather's, Gram's, Lilabet's, Raffles', and even Joshua's—Ginger saw a wonderful glow of love.

HERE COMES GINGER!

God, stop Mom's wedding!

Ginger's world is falling apart. Her mom has recently become a Christian and, even worse, has fallen in love with Grant Gabriel. Ginger can't stand the thought of leaving their little house near the beach . . . moving in with Grant and his two children . . . trading in her "brown cave of a bedroom" for a yellow canopied bed.

Ginger tries to fight the changes she knows are coming—green fingernails, salt in the sugar bowl, a near disaster at the beach. But she finds that change can happen inside her, too, when she meets the Lord her mom has come to trust.

The Ginger Series
Here Comes Ginger!   A Job for an Angel
Off to a New Start   Absolutely Green

ELAINE L. SCHULTE is a southern Californian, like Ginger. She has written many stories, articles, and books for all ages, but the **Ginger Trumbell Books** is her first series for kids.

Chariot Books™
David C. Cook Publishing Co.

A JOB FOR AN ANGEL

Love your neighbor?

October brings two new people into Ginger's life—and they couldn't be more different from each other.

Ginger looks forward to her Wednesday afternoon job of "baby-sitting" Aunt Alice. She may be elderly and ill, but she's cheerful and fun to be with. At school, however, Ginger is stuck trying to befriend grouchy Robin Lindberg, who never misses an opportunity to be nasty.

Ginger knows that "love your neighbor" includes the Robins as well as the Aunt Alices . . . but knowing doesn't make it easy. . . .

The Ginger Series
Here Comes Ginger!   A Job for an Angel
Off to a New Start   Absolutely Green

ELAINE L. SCHULTE is a southern Californian, like Ginger. She has written many stories, articles, and books for all ages, but the **Ginger Trumbell Books** is her first series for kids.

Chariot Books™
David C. Cook Publishing Co.

ABSOLUTELY GREEN

Green with envy— that's Ginger!

Life with her new "combined family" has just begun to feel natural when Ginger's mom and stepdad make an announcement: a new baby is on the way!

They sure are happy about it, but Ginger doesn't know what to think. It's clear that her stepbrother, Joshua, is anything but pleased—and for some reason, the news seems to make him grouchier than ever with Ginger.

Together Ginger's family discovers how God's love can conquer even feelings of resentment and jealousy.

The Ginger Series
 Here Comes Ginger! A Job for an Angel
 Off to a New Start Absolutely Green

ELAINE L. SCHULTE is a southern Californian, like Ginger. She has written many stories, articles, and books for all ages, but the **Ginger Trumbell Books** is her first series for kids.

Chariot Books™
David C. Cook Publishing Co.

MORE VICTORIA

Suddenly, life is nothing but problems.

Vic can see that there will be nothing dull about seventh grade . . . if she can only survive it.

First, there are the anonymous notes saying Corey Talbott, the rowdiest and most popular guy in the seventh grade has a crush on *her*. It's ridiculous, of course. But who could be writing them? And what will Vic do if Corey finds out?

Then, thanks again to the mysterious note sender, Victoria gets sent to the principal's office—the first time in her life she's faced such humiliation. What will her parents say? The last thing they need is one more thing to argue about . . . .

Live the ups and downs of Vic's first months of junior high in *More Victoria*.

Don't miss any books in The Victoria Mahoney Series!

Just Victoria

More Victoria

Take a Bow, Victoria

Only Kidding, Victoria

Maybe It's Love, Victoria

Autograph, Please, Victoria

SHELLY NIELSEN lives in Minneapolis, Minnesota, with her husband and two Yorkshire terriers.

ONLY KIDDING, VICTORIA

You've got to be kidding!

Spend the summer at a resort lodge in Minnesota . . . with her *family?* When she's been looking forward to endless days of good times with her new friends from school?

Victoria can't believe her parents are serious, but nothing she can do or say will change their minds. It's off to Little Raccoon Lake, a nowhere place where she's sure there will be nothing to do.

But the summer holds a lot of surprises—like Nina, one year older and a whole lot tougher, who scoffs at rules . . . and at Vic for bothering to keep them. And the bittersweet pang that comes with each letter from her best friend, Chelsie, reminding Vic of what she's missing back home. But the biggest surprise is Victoria's discovery of some things that have been right under her nose all along . . . .

Don't miss any books in
The Victoria Mahoney Series!

SHELLY NIELSEN lives in Minneapolis, Minnesota, with her husband and two Yorkshire terriers.

MAYBE IT'S LOVE VICTORIA

Love is mysterious.

"You never know when love is going to walk up and bop you right in the head." That's what Vic's best friend, Chelsie, says, and Chelsie usually knows. And Vic has plenty of other "mysteries" to puzzle over, too, the fall she enters eighth grade.

• How can she help Chels, who has (finally) become a Christian and expects all their friends to see and care about the big change in her life?

• How can she keep her crazy grandmother's wedding from becoming a three-ring circus (complete with a bridesmaid's dress that makes Vic look like a bumblebee)?

• And how is she supposed to figure out this crazy thing called love?

Vic's faith in God grows as together she and Chelsie weather another season of junior high.

Don't miss any books in The Victoria Mahoney Series!

Just Victoria	Only Kidding, Victoria
More Victoria	Maybe It's Love, Victoria
Take a Bow, Victoria	Autograph, Please, Victoria

SHELLY NIELSEN lives in Minneapolis, Minnesota, with her husband and two Yorkshire terriers.